"What are you looki~~ng~~ in a woman?"

Sabena asked.

"I'm not looking."

"You know what I mean. What would your ideal woman be like?"

Jake's gaze swept over her finely modeled features. "She'd have big blue eyes and hair as shining as a raven's wing."

"Why won't you tell me?"

"What difference can it possibly make to you?" he countered.

"I'm merely trying to understand you. Why are you so wary?"

"When I was a little boy, my mother read me the story of Samson and Delilah. It made quite an impression."

"I don't think she meant you to take it so literally. Besides, you have nothing to worry about. Just stay away from women barbers."

"A man always has to worry about a clever woman. She can make him believe in fairy tales."

Dear Reader,

Welcome to Silhouette **Special Edition** . . . welcome to romance. Each month, Silhouette **Special Edition** publishes six novels with you in mind—stories of love and life, tales that you can identify with . . . as well as dream about.

We're starting off the New Year right in 1993. We're pleased to announce our new series, THAT SPECIAL WOMAN! Each month, we'll be presenting a book that pays tribute to women—to us. The heroine is a friend, a wife, a mother—a striver, a nurturer, a pursuer of goals—she's the best in every woman. And it takes a very special man to win that special woman! Launching this series is *Building Dreams* by Ginna Gray. Ryan McCall doesn't know what he's up against when he meets Tess Benson in this compelling tale. She's a woman after the cynical builder's heart—and she won't stop until she's got her man!

On the horizon this month, too, is MAVERICKS, a new series by Lisa Jackson. *He's a Bad Boy* introduces three men who just won't be tamed!

Rounding out the month are more stories from other favorite authors—Tracy Sinclair, Christine Flynn, Kayla Daniels and Judith Bowen (with her first Silhouette **Special Edition** title!).

I hope that you enjoy this book and all the stories to come. Happy 1993!

Sincerely,

Tara Gavin
Senior Editor
Silhouette Books

TRACY SINCLAIR

THE CAT THAT LIVED ON PARK AVENUE

Silhouette®

SPECIAL EDITION®

Published by Silhouette Books New York

America's Publisher of Contemporary Romance

SILHOUETTE BOOKS
300 East 42nd St., New York, N.Y. 10017

THE CAT THAT LIVED ON PARK AVENUE

Copyright © 1993 by Tracy Sinclair

All rights reserved. Except for use in any review, the reproduction
or utilization of this work in whole or in part in any form by any
electronic, mechanical or other means, now known or hereafter
invented, including xerography, photocopying and recording, or in
any information storage or retrieval system, is forbidden without
the permission of the publisher, Silhouette Books, 300 E. 42nd St.,
New York, N.Y. 10017

ISBN: 0-373-09791-3

First Silhouette Books printing January 1993

All the characters in this book have no existence outside the
imagination of the author and have no relation whatsoever to
anyone bearing the same name or names. They are not even
distantly inspired by any individual known or unknown to the
author, and all incidents are pure invention.

®: Trademark used under license and registered in the United
States Patent and Trademark Office and in other countries.

Printed in the U.S.A.

Books by Tracy Sinclair

Silhouette Special Edition

Never Give Your Heart #12
Mixed Blessing #34
Designed for Love #52
Castles in the Air #68
Fair Exchange #105
Winter of Love #140
The Tangled Web #153
The Harvest Is Love #183
Pride's Folly #208
Intrigue in Venice #232
A Love So Tender #249
Dream Girl #287
Preview of Paradise #309
Forgive and Forget #355
Mandrego #386
No Room for Doubt #421
More Precious than Jewels #453
Champagne for Breakfast #481
Proof Positive #493
Sky High #512
King of Hearts #531
Miss Robinson Crusoe #565
Willing Partners #584
Golden Adventure #605
The Girl Most Likely To #619
A Change of Place #672
The Man She Married #701
If the Truth Be Told #725
Dreamboat of the Western World #746
The Cat That Lived on Park Avenue #791

Silhouette Romance

Paradise Island #39
Holiday in Jamaica #123
Flight to Romance #174
Stars in Her Eyes #244
Catch a Rising Star #345
Love Is Forever #459
Anything But Marriage #892

Silhouette Books

Silhouette Christmas Stories 1986
"Under the Mistletoe"

TRACY SINCLAIR,

author of more than thirty Silhouette novels, also contributes to various magazines and newspapers. An extensive traveler and a dedicated volunteer worker, this California resident has accumulated countless fascinating experiences, settings and acquaintances to draw on in plotting her romances.

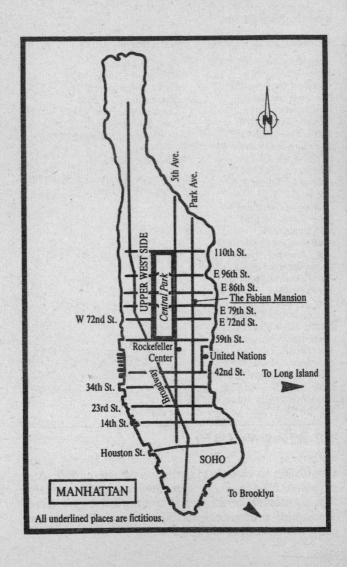

5th Ave.

Park Ave.

110th St.

E 96th St.

UPPER WEST SIDE

E 86th St.

<u>The Fabian Mansion</u>

Central Park

E 79th St.

E 72nd St.

W 72nd St.

59th St.

Rockefeller
Center

United Nations

42nd St.

To Long Island

Broadway

34th St.

23rd St.

14th St.

Houston St.

SOHO

To Brooklyn

MANHATTAN

All underlined places are fictitious.

Chapter One

Sabena Murphy didn't look like a private detective. She had long black hair, sapphire-blue eyes framed by sooty lashes and a figure that made old men feel young again. Nobody would have guessed she was the head of her own agency.

The decision to go it alone was risky, but she wanted more exciting cases than those of industrial espionage and corporate leaks she'd been assigned at Worldwide Investigations.

Business hadn't exactly been brisk so far, but one morning she received a telephone call that sounded promising. A woman asked to see her about a very urgent matter. She gave an address on Park Avenue.

A short time later, Sabena stood on the sidewalk outside an imposing old brick mansion. Please let this be more than just a sleazy divorce case, she begged silently.

The woman who answered the door allayed Sabena's fears somewhat. She had short gray hair and a still-trim figure despite her age, which was probably around sixty something.

"You must be Miss Murphy." The woman extended her hand. "I'm Martha Lambert. Come in, please."

The inside of the house was as elegant as the outside had promised. Sabena had a swift impression of polished floors, oriental area rugs, and paintings in heavy gold frames. Before she could make a more detailed inspection, something black streaked across the entryway and disappeared into the shadowy hall beyond.

"What was that?" she gasped.

"A black cat. He's one of the reasons I require your services." Martha's expression was a mixture of grimness and amusement at Sabena's puzzled face.

She led the way to a pleasant room that was a combination office and sitting room. A large carved desk was positioned in front of the long French windows, but the furnishings also included a chintz-covered sofa and several comfortable chairs.

After they were seated, Martha said, "I've never met a private detective before, but for some reason I thought you'd be older."

"I've had a lot of experience," Sabena assured her earnestly. "I worked for Worldwide Investigations for three years. The only reason I left was that I wanted to start my own agency. They were very satisfied with my work. You can check with them."

"I'll take your word for it." The woman's shrewd eyes evaluated her. "I've always relied on my own judgment about people, and I think you're just the person I'm looking for."

"I'll certainly try to justify your confidence." Sabena stared at her curiously. "How did you happen to pick me?"

Martha's smile was surprisingly youthful. "I had a boyfriend in high school named Murphy. When I saw your ad in the Yellow Pages, it triggered old memories. Another attraction was your lack of hyperbole. Those advertisements placed by the large agencies are so strident," she said distastefully.

For the first time, Sabena blessed the tight budget that had prompted her to place such a modest ad. "What kind of services are you looking for?" she asked.

"I want you to find a cat."

Sabena's hopes plunged. This was almost worse than shadowing a cheating husband. Sabena Murphy, tracer of lost animals, she thought sardonically.

Her expression wasn't lost on Martha. "Perhaps you won't be so disappointed when you hear the whole story. Lucky is no ordinary cat."

"I'm sure he means a lot to you," Sabena said politely.

"You could say he's worth millions," Martha answered wryly. "But not to me. I'd better start at the beginning. Perhaps you've heard of Katherine Fabian?"

The name was familiar. Sabena searched her memory and remembered the fabulously wealthy spinster who had died several weeks ago. The newspapers had had a field day with the story.

"She was the one who left her entire fortune to her cat."

"Not exactly," Martha corrected. "She made large bequests to charity, took excellent care of her servants and made me independent for life. I was her secretary-companion for over twenty years."

"But the bulk of her estate went to the cat."

"Again, that's not quite accurate. Katherine's will stated that Lucky was to live in this house for the rest of his natural life. After his demise, her relatives—two sisters, a brother and a great-niece—will inherit the entire estate."

"I didn't read that part," Sabena said slowly.

"No, of course not. It doesn't make as good a story," Martha replied disdainfully. "The tabloids preferred to portray Katherine as a senile old woman, but I can assure you, she was in full possession of her faculties."

"You must admit it was a rather unusual will," Sabena pointed out carefully.

"Admittedly, Katherine was eccentric. She could afford to be. But she was a brilliant woman. Let me tell you something about the Fabian family. Katherine took a modest inheritance and built it into a fortune, unlike her siblings who mostly squandered their resources. They're all comfortable, however. One sister, Marguerite, got handsome settlements from three husbands. She's still a beautiful woman, but a total airhead. I think her spouses were glad to pay to get rid of her, although she'll probably marry again. Unlike her sister, Harriet, who's so sour she makes your mouth pucker."

"Then I don't suppose Harriet is married."

"She was, but her husband died some years ago. He was completely under her thumb at home, poor soul, but successful in business. He left Harriet well provided for."

"How about Miss Fabian's brother and great-niece?" Sabena asked. "Are they well off, also?"

"Not like the sisters. Charles Fabian is an aging playboy who has turned sponging off of other people into a fine art," Martha said crisply. "He will always find someone to subsidize him. I regret having to be so blunt, but the circumstances demand frankness. They aren't an appealing family."

"Including the niece?"

"No, I shouldn't have lumped Emily in with the rest. She's really a very nice girl. Katherine was fond of her. I think Marguerite resented their close relationship."

"Why is that?"

"Marguerite is Emily's grandmother, although she insists that the girl call her by her first name. Did you ever hear of anything so ridiculous? Marguerite refuses to admit she'd old enough to be a grandmother."

Sabena was trying to sort out the relationships. "Then, Emily's mother or father was Marguerite's daughter or son."

"Daughter. She and her husband were killed in a tragic automobile accident some years ago."

"Emily must be quite young."

"Yes, she's in her early twenties."

"What are the state of *her* finances?"

"Emily has a good job as a junior curator at the Metropolitan Museum. She's also engaged to a well-placed young stockbroker."

"But she isn't as affluent as the others?"

"I suppose that's a fair assessment," Martha admitted grudgingly. "But it won't be a hardship for any of them to wait for their inheritance."

"Still, the will must have been a big disappointment to all of them. Are they contesting it?"

"They seemed to accept the terms at first, although they hired an attorney named Jake Waring—in a purely advisory capacity, supposedly. A clause in Katherine's will states that anyone who contests the provisions will be automatically disinherited."

Sabena's eyes narrowed in thought. "There's an easier way than litigation. What if Lucky used up all of his nine lives."

"Katherine didn't overlook that possibility. If Lucky should die from other than natural causes, *all* of the heirs are to be disinherited. This was to insure that one of them couldn't take the blame and have the others chip in to make up his or her share."

"Then I don't see what the problem is," Sabena remarked. "Miss Fabian seems to have covered all bases."

"All except one. Lucky has disappeared."

"But I just saw him!" Sabena exclaimed.

"No, you saw his replacement."

"I don't understand."

"The first thing the Fabian's attorney did was to have Lucky paw-printed. Mr. Waring was quite candid about the reason. He said if Lucky should happen to die, I could substitute another cat in his place without anyone being the wiser. Which of course is true," Martha said matter-of-factly. "One black cat looks very similar to another, except to its owner."

"Why would you bother, though? As I understand it, you and the charities get your bequests up front. Lucky's longevity—or lack of it—doesn't affect you."

"That's not strictly true. Katherine realized it wasn't enough to stipulate that Lucky was to have a home here for life. Somebody responsible had to keep an eye on him. She named me as that person—with a proviso. If for any reason I'm unwilling or unable, I'm supposed to choose someone reliable to take my place."

Sabena gazed at her speculatively. "How old is Lucky?"

"About four or five. He was quite young when Katherine rescued him from traffic, but the veterinarian was unable to tell his precise age."

"Cats can live to be as much as fourteen, can't they?" Sabena asked.

"Or even older."

"So it's possible that you could stay on here for a very long time."

"Now you're thinking like Mr. Waring," Martha said dryly. "Yes, I could live here comfortably for many years. But I don't want to—in spite of what the heirs believe. I feel a responsibility to carry out Katherine's wishes. She was my friend as well as my employer. But I never wanted to remain here without her. I'd like to buy a house in the country and do all the things I've never had time for—gardening, cooking, taking long, aimless walks. After I found someone trustworthy to take over for me, that's what I planned to do. Now everything is up in the air. Lucky has to be found."

"I'd like to take the case, but I have to be honest with you," Sabena said. "If one of the heirs made off with Lucky, he or she probably disposed of him immediately."

"I don't think so. They wouldn't take a chance until the money was actually distributed. In case of an unforeseen slipup."

"Like what?"

"If the abduction was traced to one of the heirs and he couldn't produce Lucky unharmed, they'd all be disinherited."

"If the cat disappeared mysteriously, isn't it safe to assume that he's dead?"

"A good lawyer could claim that he just wandered off. And I can assure you, Jake Waring is a *very* good lawyer."

"Even so, isn't the fact that the cats were switched proof enough that Lucky met with foul play?" Sabena argued.

"It throws suspicion on me more than the heirs. That's what makes the whole plot so diabolical." Martha's face was troubled. "I'll be under a cloud for the rest of my life, and whoever did this rotten thing will get away with it. The court won't tie up the estate indefinitely with so much money involved." She sighed. "I've let Katherine down terribly."

"You couldn't anticipate anything like this," Sabena consoled her.

"I could scarcely believe it. I hoped with all my heart that I was mistaken when I began to suspect this cat wasn't Lucky."

"What tipped off the lawyer?" Sabena asked curiously.

"I don't know. He just showed up here one day with the whole family, and said they wanted another set of prints."

"Didn't you think that was rather strange?"

"This entire affair is bizarre! The only chance I have to clear my name is to find Lucky as soon as possible. His life is over the minute that money is distributed."

"Don't give up now. We haven't even begun to fight back." Sabena's smile expressed more confidence than she felt.

"Do you really think you can find him?"

"I'm going to give it my best shot. First of all, I'll need some background information on each of the relatives, plus a physical description."

The doorbell rang and Martha said, "You can judge the last part for yourself. I've asked the family to come here today."

"How did you get them to agree? I imagine relations between you are rather strained."

"I told them I'd found some jewelry of Katherine's that hadn't been mentioned in the will. That eased the strain considerably."

"Was the story true?" Sabena asked uncertainly.

"Certainly. I have no reason to lie."

"Shouldn't you have turned whatever you found over to the attorney for the estate?"

Martha smiled. "It's costume jewelry, but I'm sure her sisters and brother are salivating at the thought of—" She broke off abruptly as a man appeared in the doorway.

Sabena glanced over, her initial interest turning to surprise. This man couldn't be Miss Fabian's brother. He was young, somewhere in his thirties, with the tall, broad-shouldered physique of an athlete. Everything about him spelled money, his elegant dark suit and maroon Hermès tie, his expensively cut hair. He must be Emily's stockbroker fiancé.

Martha dispelled that notion when she remarked, "I didn't expect to see you here today, Mr. Waring."

"I hope you don't mind," he answered urbanely. "One of my clients phoned and suggested I be present."

Martha nodded. "That would be Harriet, no doubt."

Without denying or confirming her surmise, the attorney glanced at Sabena. His unusual hazel eyes were more golden than green, giving her the fleeting impression of a sleek and dangerous tiger. Sabena was used to arousing male interest, but the comprehensive look he gave her was unsettling. Jake Waring would be a formidable adversary—in the courtroom or out of it.

Martha followed his gaze. "This is Sabena Murphy, the daughter of a dear friend of mine. She's visiting from out of town."

Sabena admired her inventiveness on such short notice, but she wished they'd had time to get together on their stories. Especially when Jake pursued the subject.

"Where are you from, Miss Murphy?"

He was very observant. A quick look at her left hand had told him she was unmarried. "A little town in Wisconsin," Sabena answered. "You wouldn't have heard of it."

"Try me."

"Pear Blossom." It was the first name that popped into her mind.

"How unusual. I didn't know they grew pears in Wisconsin."

"What's in a name?" she asked airily. "I'm sure all the people in Los Angeles aren't angels."

"Funny you should mention California. They have a Pear Blossom there, too, if I'm not mistaken."

That was where she'd gotten the name! A submerged memory from her childhood on the West Coast. Why was he interested in her background, though? Maybe it was just a lawyer's natural impulse to cross-examine.

"Would you like some coffee, Mr. Waring?" Martha asked swiftly.

"If it's not too much trouble."

"No trouble at all. I'll tell Greta to bring in a tray."

As she moved to a silken bellpull by the draperies at the front windows, Jake asked Sabena, "Where are you staying?"

Before she was forced to answer, Martha announced, "Marguerite and Harriet are here."

The doorbell rang and a moment later two women were shown into the sitting room. They were within a few years of each other, but the similarity ended there.

Marguerite was still very attractive. Skillful plastic surgery had given her a wrinkle-free face, and dieting had maintained an excellent figure. Her blond hair was undoubtedly colored but expertly so.

Harriet was Marguerite's direct opposite. She was plain and stout, and her dark hair was sprinkled with gray. A thin mouth and permanent frown lines gave a clue to her personality.

"What's all this about jewelry?" she asked Martha without preamble. "Why weren't we told about its existence before?"

"How nice of you to come, Harriet," Martha answered ironically. "Hello, Marguerite. Won't you sit down? Coffee will be here in a moment."

"Don't change the subject," Harriet ordered. "Very strange things are happening around here. If things aren't *dis*appearing, they're *re*appearing. You're either incompetent or dishonest."

Martha's eyes glinted dangerously. "Since you asked your attorney to be present today, perhaps you'd better have him advise you on the penalty for slander."

"I suggest we all calm down, ladies," Jake said. "Marguerite, you're looking especially lovely today. Is that a new hairstyle?"

She expanded under his compliment. As any woman would, Sabena thought sardonically. Jake Waring could charm a hanging judge—if she were female. But underneath that polish and sophistication, Sabena sensed a tough-as-nails street fighter. She didn't trust him for a second.

Marguerite was patting her coiffure complacently. "I found a new hairdresser. Do you really like it?"

"What difference does it make?" Harriet snapped. "We came to see Katherine's jewelry, not so you could make a fool of yourself over a man half your age."

"I happen to prefer younger men. They have such marvelous staying power." Marguerite smiled mischievously.

"That's disgusting!" her sister said.

"Poor Harriet, it must be dreadful to be so repressed," Marguerite mused. "A good healthy sex life would make all the difference in your personality."

Harriet's face turned a mottled red. "I consider that remark in extremely poor taste."

As Jake struggled to conceal his amusement, the housekeeper brought in a large silver tray bearing an ornate coffee service and a tea stand filled with cookies. While Martha was pouring, Charles Fabian, the brother, arrived. He was a distinguished-looking man with silver temples and the ingratiating manner of a snake-oil salesman. Sabena had to agree with Martha's appraisal of the family. They weren't anything to brag about.

Charles immediately targeted Sabena. "And who is this young charmer?"

Harriet barely waited for Martha to make the introductions before demanding again to see the jewelry. "This isn't a social occasion," she stared.

"I thought we'd wait for Emily," Martha said.

"Is that necessary?" Harriet asked Jake.

He shrugged. "She's one of the heirs."

"Then she should be on time like the rest of us."

"I don't think our waiting a few more minutes would be unreasonable," he said mildly.

"Sure, *you're* getting paid for your time," Harriet muttered. "You don't care if we spend all day here."

Jake's high cheekbones seemed to sharpen, but his voice remained pleasant. "You were the one who asked me to come here today, Mrs. Sheridan. I really don't know why."

"To protect our interests. That's why we're paying you that outrageous retainer. I want you to make sure Martha turns everything over to us."

"I can't do that. The jewelry is part of the estate."

"Katherine must have meant for us to have it," Harriet insisted.

"That's a matter for..." Jake intercepted the amused look Martha cast at Sabena. "Why don't we reserve judgment for now?"

Emily arrived a few moments later, like a breath of fresh air. A strong family resemblance to her grandmother was evident, although Emily's long straight hair was light brown, and her unlined skin was due to youth, not the expertise of a plastic surgeon.

"Sorry I'm late. I had a terrible time getting a cab." Her eyes widened when she glanced around the room and saw Jake. "What's up? Has Lucky been found?"

"That silly cat is gone for good," Marguerite said. "I don't know why the court won't admit it and give us our money. I've already made plans to leave for Europe."

Since she addressed the last part of her remark to Jake, he said, "It isn't quite that simple."

Harriet's mouth thinned even more. "Lawyers like to drag things out so they can justify their fat fees."

Sabena wondered when Jake's patience was going to run out. It would take a man of steel not to snap back under that kind of provocation. But when his eyes met hers with amused comprehension, she realized this was no ordinary man. She couldn't imagine him losing control—not even when making love. It was impossible to picture that hard mouth softening in a kiss, or whispering tender endearments.

Sabena's delicate skin colored. She looked away swiftly, with the uncomfortable feeling that he was reading her mind.

"Will you please stop your sniping?" Marguerite told her sister. "Jake is on our side, remember?"

"I haven't seen any results," Harriet answered stubbornly.

"He discovered the cats were switched," Charles reminded her. "Although I must agree with you on one point. I don't see what's holding up our money. Katherine's cat is history."

"That's right. What are you waiting for—the catnapper to send us one of the little beast's ears?" Harriet asked Jake sarcastically.

"I sincerely hope not." He gazed back at her calmly. "That would prove he'd been destroyed. In which case, none of you would inherit a dime."

The sisters and brother looked at one another in alarm. Charles spoke for all of them. "Hold on a moment! We all know he simply ran away. Cats are notoriously stupid, but Martha isn't. She substituted another animal so she could freeload here for another ten years or more."

As Martha glanced significantly at Sabena, Harriet sneered, "If anyone knows about freeloading, it's you, Charles."

"Whose side are *you* on?" he asked indignantly.

Emily put her hands over her ears. "I don't want to hear any more! Is this what you dragged me away from work for?"

"The child is correct," Marguerite said. "We're all in this together, for better or worse."

Did she mean that literally, Sabena wondered? It wouldn't make her job easy.

"We came to see Katherine's jewelry," Marguerite continued, her eyes sparkling in anticipation.

"What jewelry?" Emily asked blankly.

"That's what we're going to find out," Harriet said. "Unless Martha has some further delaying tactics."

"On the contrary." Martha rose and went to the desk. After unlocking a bottom drawer, she took out a large leather jewelry box. Placing it on top of the desk, she smiled. "I'm very anxious to have you see what's in here."

The three older people jostled one another getting to the desk. Marguerite was the quickest. She threw open the cover of the box and stared avidly at the contents, a collection of brooches, rings and bracelets.

Her expression changed when she began lifting out various pieces. "This is *costume* jewelry!"

Harriet's face was a study in frustration. "It's nothing but junk."

"Don't be too hasty." Charles studied a pin that was set with deep red stones. "These might be rubies."

"They're garnets," Martha said. "I gave Katherine that brooch."

"You knew these things were fake!" Marguerite turned on her furiously. "You deliberately got our hopes up for nothing."

"This was the jewelry Katherine wore every day. I thought it might have sentimental value for you," Martha answered evenly.

Emily approached the desk for the first time. "I'd like to have the little gold locket she always wore." She looked questioningly at Jake. "Would that be all right?"

His rugged face softened. "I didn't know Miss Fabian, but I'm sure she'd want you to have it."

Sabena found herself wishing he'd look at *her* that way, then chastised herself for the fleeting thought. Jake Waring was being paid to thwart her efforts at every turn, and she'd better not forget it.

Harriet was pawing around in the contents of the box. "I guess I could use these onyx earrings."

"People aren't wearing their real jewelry except on special occasions." Marguerite held up the garnet brooch. "This stuff might come in handy, after all."

The mixture of disgust and sadness in Martha's eyes was painful. Sabena turned away and went to pour herself another cup of coffee.

"Wills have a way of bringing out the worst in people," a low voice remarked.

Jake was standing next to her, watching her with almost the same compassion he'd shown Emily. Sabena reacted instinctively, warming to him. Why had she thought he was unfeeling?

"Did you know Katherine Fabian well?" he asked.

Sabena glanced down at her cup. "No, I never met her."

"I see."

The odd note in his voice made her look up swiftly. The moment of rapport was gone. Jake's golden eyes were watchful. They were adversaries once more, although his suave manner was meant to conceal the fact.

"You were so upset just now," he commented. "I thought perhaps you'd also given Miss Fabian some of that jewelry."

"I was upset because of Martha. She really cared about Katherine. It's breaking her heart to watch those vultures dismiss their sister's prized possessions as worthless! Whatever happened to sentiment?"

"You must admit Martha deliberately led them on," Jake answered mildly. His gaze sharpened. "You knew the box contained costume jewelry, didn't you?"

Sabena met his eyes squarely. "I never saw that box before today."

Emily joined them, wearing the gold locket. She held it out to show them. "Isn't it lovely? I'm going to put Aunt Katherine's picture in one side, and Don's in the other. My fiancé," she explained to Sabena.

"It's beautiful," Sabena told her. "I hope you get a lot of pleasure out of it."

Emily looked hesitantly at Jake. "I don't want to start a big donnybrook, but I think Martha should have a keepsake, too."

"I agree with you," he said.

"Could you talk them into it? Aunt Harriet and the others are bound to throw a major tantrum if I suggest it, even though there isn't any significant amount of money involved."

He smiled. "What makes you think they'll listen to me?"

Emily grinned mischievously. "I don't think you're a man who gets turned down very often."

"I'm not quite sure how to take that," he said with amusement.

"You know what I mean. You're the only one who can keep them in line. They're convinced that Martha is responsible for the will, but if you knew Aunt Katherine, you'd know that *nobody* could influence her."

"You don't feel any hostility toward Martha?" Sabena asked. "Even though she benefited and you didn't?"

"I can understand my family's feelings," Emily replied carefully. "They're a lot older than I, so it's more difficult for them to wait for the money. But I don't think any of us should resent Martha. She was very loyal to Aunt Katherine for many years."

"Then you can't think she would switch the cats," Sabena said.

Jake stepped in. "What Emily thinks is totally irrelevant. It's a matter for the courts to decide."

Emily looked at him gratefully. "I have to make a quick phone call, and then I must get back to work."

As she left them, Sabena crumbled a cookie unobtrusively. Setting her cup on the tray, she displayed her sticky fingers. "I'd better go wash my hands."

Jake delayed her. "You aren't an attorney, by any chance, are you, Miss Murphy?"

She looked at him warily. "No. Why do you ask?"

"That was a nice cross-examination you were subjecting Emily to."

"I notice you stopped me," Sabena answered coolly. "Were you afraid she was going to say something incriminating?"

"That sounds as if you think she has something to hide," he countered. "What do you suspect her of?"

Sabena realized a direct confrontation would be useless. Her original plan of listening in on Emily's conversation was more apt to be fruitful.

"I have no reason to suspect her of anything," she said. "I'm only interested in convincing all of you that

Martha isn't guilty of anything, either. Now, if you'll excuse me, I really want to wash my hands." She walked away, conscious of Jake's eyes following her.

An alcove in the shadowy hall held a telephone. Emily was talking on it, her back to the sitting room.

"I didn't see any reason to," she was saying. "Why should you come all the way from downtown? I wouldn't have come myself if I'd known what it was all about. Marguerite wouldn't tell me, but she was so excited, I thought maybe Lucky had turned up."

Sabena flattened herself against the wall and remained absolutely motionless.

"No, I agree," Emily responded to the other person's remark. After a pause, "Who knows? We'll just have to wait and see. I doubt if anyone will ever trace him. We—" She turned around and discovered she wasn't alone.

Sabena moved away from the wall at the same instant. "I was looking for the powder room."

"Right in there." Emily indicated a door a short distance away.

Sabena smiled her thanks and walked past her. She closed the door audibly, then opened it a crack, being careful not to make a sound.

Emily went back to her conversation. "Just a friend of Martha's." Her tone changed to impatience at the reply. "Don't start that again, Don. You have to feel sorry for Martha. Nobody is ever going to believe she didn't do it."

Sabena felt her pulse quicken the way it always did when a break in a case seemed imminent. Though it was too soon to jump to conclusions, Emily's conversation with her fiancé was very provocative. What was Emily about to say after, "I doubt if anyone will ever trace him."? "We put him where nobody will ever find him? We buried his body in Central Park?" What? It was too bad Emily had to turn around just then.

Sabena's excitement was tempered by regret that Emily was the likely culprit. Any of her relatives would be preferable. Emily had seemed so gentle and caring. Then Sabena remembered the sweet old ladies who poisoned their lodgers for their social security checks. She put her ear to the door again, but Emily was almost finished with her conversation.

"I really have to get back to work, Don. We'll talk tonight... Don't tell me you forgot! We're going to that gallery showing... McConnell's on East Fifty-seventh Street. Meet me there at seven-thirty. I love you."

Sabena closed the bathroom door silently. She turned on the water and washed her hands. By the time she returned to the sitting room, Emily had gone. All the others were still there, however, including Jake. He was talking to Martha, who looked gratified.

"That's very kind of you," she said as Sabena joined them. "I *would* like something of Katherine's to remember her by."

"I'd say she left you quite a lot," he answered dryly.

Martha gave him a rueful look. "And I was beginning to like you."

Just don't trust him, Sabena thought silently. Jake was an enigma. He could be unexpectedly kind, and then turn around and be as hard as steel.

They were interrupted by a sharp question from Harriet. "Where's the mate to this earring?"

When Martha left them to answer Harriet's imperious summons, Jake looked at his watch. "It's almost noon," he commented.

"Time sure flies when you're having fun," Sabena remarked ironically.

"Perhaps I can make the rest of the day more enjoyable for you. Will you have lunch with me?"

Sabena didn't doubt that it would be enjoyable—or at least, eventful. But she questioned his motives. "Why would you want to take me to lunch?"

His eyes took on that tiger glow as he gazed at her soft lips. "Don't you have any mirrors in your house?"

"Several, but that doesn't answer my question. Try to be truthful, please," she said crisply. "I'm not as trusting as I look."

"You *look* like an angelic blue-eyed innocent, but I never thought you were," he answered calmly.

Sabena was caught between indignation and laughter. "I think I've just been insulted, but the sugarcoating is so thick, I can't be sure."

"I have many faults, but insulting women isn't among them. I try to be very gentle with women."

Her active imagination supplied the details his deep velvet voice implied. Jake would be an expert lover, knowing when to hold his superb body in check, and the right moment to release its power.

"So you see, it's quite safe to have lunch with me." He smiled at her dazzled face.

Sabena felt her cheeks grow warm with embarrassment. Did Jake guess that she was speculating about his expertise? Not necessarily. He simply knew what effect he had on women.

She drew a deep breath. "Safe, but still puzzling. You obviously can tell that my sympathies are with Martha, not your clients."

"I wasn't proposing a business lunch. You have nothing to do with the case, do you?"

"How could I?" she asked, just as smoothly. "I just arrived in town."

"That's right. From Pear Blossom. Are you staying with Martha?"

"No, I'm not."

Although he waited expectantly, Sabena didn't satisfy his curiosity. If only she'd had a chance to prepare a cover story before he and the others were sprung on her. This way, she had to wing it, and that was dangerous with a man like Jake.

"We've gotten off the subject of lunch," he said. "What's your answer?"

Sabena hesitated. It made sense to stay in contact with Jake. He could give her valuable information about the Fabian family.

She really needed to talk to her client first, however. At this point, Jake knew more about Martha than *she* did. A misstep would give her away.

"I have a date with Martha for lunch," Sabena said reluctantly.

"I understand. Perhaps some other time. How long are you staying?"

"A couple of weeks." The case promised to take that long, at least.

"Then I'm sure we'll run into each other again," he said pleasantly.

Sabena saw him slipping away. Suddenly she thought of a way to cover two bases at once. "If you're not busy tonight, there's a gallery show I'd love to see."

"Really? Where is it?"

"At McConnell's on East Fifty-seventh Street."

His golden eyes were unreadable. "For someone who just arrived in New York, you're remarkably well informed about events and locations."

Belatedly, Sabena realized she'd revealed too much familiarity with the city. The damage wasn't irreparable, however.

Her face was a picture of innocence as she gazed up at him. "Emily happened to mention where it was being held. I'd really like to go." She gave a tinkling little laugh. "We don't have gallery shows in Pear Blossom."

"Then we can't have you miss this one. I'd be happy to take you."

"Great! Will seven-thirty be convenient?"

"That sounds fine. We'll have dinner afterward. What hotel are you staying at?"

She thought rapidly. "I'm not. A girlfriend was kind enough to offer me her apartment while she's out of town."

"I hope it isn't in Brooklyn," he said ruefully.

"No, it's here in Manhattan."

"Good. What's the address?"

"You don't have to pick me up. I'll meet you at the gallery."

"Even in New York, a gentleman calls for his date."

"This isn't a date," she protested. "*I* asked *you.*"

"I fail to see the relevance of that fact. Isn't that still called a date in Pear Blossom?" he teased.

Sabena sidestepped the question. "It really would be more convenient if I met you there." Before he could ask why, she glanced over at the others. "I wish they'd hurry up and leave. I'd like to spend some time with Martha."

Jake looked at his watch. "And I have phone calls to make."

The gathering broke up when Jake announced he was leaving. Was it possible that he was the mastermind behind the plot to undermine Katherine's will? It seemed farfetched. Jake was a well-known lawyer. And yet . . . The heirs would be very grateful to anyone who arranged for them to get their money.

"I'm looking forward to tonight," he told Sabena as he shepherded his group out the door. "It should be very interesting."

"I was thinking the same thing," she answered demurely.

Chapter Two

"I hope it was worth the ordeal," Martha said wearily as the door closed behind the Fabian family. "Did you find out anything useful?"

"I got some interesting impressions—of them *and* their attorney."

"Yes, I heard him say he'd see you tonight," Martha said dryly.

"It's purely business," Sabena assured her.

The older woman wasn't convinced. "He's a handsome devil."

"And very clever. How much do you know about Jake Waring?"

"He's a prominent attorney. I've seen his name in the paper in connection with important cases. He usually wins them."

"I got the impression that coming in first is very important to Jake," Sabena said thoughtfully. "I wonder how far he'd go to win a case."

"I'm not sure what you're driving at."

"He could get rich on this one case alone," Sabena speculated aloud.

"Do you really believe he'd jeopardize a prestigious career for the sake of money?" Martha asked.

"I only said it's feasible. At this point, everyone is a suspect."

"I can't see Emily as a candidate. She was always fond of Lucky. She's also a very sweet girl. Fortunately the only thing she seems to have inherited from her grandmother is Marguerite's looks."

Sabena didn't tell Martha about the conversation she'd overheard. "I need to know everything you can tell me about the people involved, including yourself. Jake might ask questions tonight, to see if I really am the daughter of a friend."

"You don't think he believed me?" Martha asked.

"I don't think he takes anything or anybody on faith," Sabena answered crisply. "I want to be prepared when I go up against him."

"I'll tell Greta to serve lunch. This might take quite a while."

"How long has Greta worked here?" Sabena asked, after the servant had come and gone.

"Longer than I have," Martha replied. "The Swensons were here when I was hired. Greta cooks and does light housekeeping, and her husband, Lars, does the heavy work. He also acted as Katherine's chauffeur."

"Do they plan to retire once they get their bequests?"

"They intended to stay on as long as Lucky was alive. This has been their home for so many years. Now, I suppose they'll have to leave. I imagine the house will be sold and the proceeds divided among the heirs."

"So, Greta and Lars would have no reason to do away with Lucky," Sabena mused. "Unless someone made it extremely worth their while."

"I'm sure they're above suspicion," Martha protested.

"Nobody is above suspicion."

Before Martha could argue further, Greta returned to tell them lunch was ready.

The breakfast room where the table was set overlooked a small garden. Flowers bloomed in beds bordering the enclosing brick wall, and a flagstone patio held outdoor furniture.

"This is charming," Sabena exclaimed. "What a luxury to have a real garden in the middle of the city."

"Yes, Katherine and I enjoyed eating out here on sunny days."

As they were gazing at the view, the black cat streaked past them and disappeared through a pet door just above floor level.

Sabena jumped visibly. "He seems awfully frightened of people."

"Just the opposite of Lucky." Martha sighed. "Lucky would go to anybody. That was his undoing, no doubt."

Sabena watched as the cat returned through the pet door he had just exited. "I'm surprised this one hasn't run away."

"It's probably the first time the poor little stray has been fed regularly."

Sabena looked thoughtful. "Is there a way into the garden from outside?"

"There's a door in the wall. Deliveries are made to a tradesman's entrance, where there's a bell. The rest of the time, the door is kept locked. Lars is the only other person who uses it, mostly when he carts out the trash."

"Where is the key kept?" Sabena asked.

"On a hook in the kitchen. But I'm sure it isn't missing. He or Greta would have told me."

"I don't doubt that it's still there. A wax impression could have been taken, however."

"This all sounds so cloak-and-daggerish," Martha said helplessly.

"People have gone to more trouble for a lot less."

Over lunch, Martha told a slightly different story than Sabena expected. For some reason, she'd thought Martha was a spinster like Katherine.

"I met my future husband in college," she began. "We were married right after graduation. Except for the fact that we were unable to have children, life was very good to me. That all came to an end when Fred died of a heart attack, just after his fortieth birthday."

"How very sad," Sabena murmured.

Martha nodded. "When I got over my grief and shock, I had to think about supporting myself. I wasn't destitute, but Fred died too young to have left much of an estate. The problem was, I had never worked for a living. I'm not counting the summer vacation jobs while I was in college. Those were all temporary unskilled jobs."

"You never worked after you were married?" Sabena asked.

"Times were different then. Women didn't work unless they had to. I was perfectly happy being a housewife." Martha slanted a defensive glance at her. "I suppose that seems reprehensible to you."

"Not at all. I believe everybody should do what's right for them without being criticized for it."

The older woman looked gratified. "I'd taken typing and shorthand in school," she continued. "But I soon discovered employers weren't waiting with open arms for a forty-year-old woman with no experience. I was getting a little panicky when I answered Katherine's ad."

"She must have had a lot of applicants."

"Dozens of them, but we clicked immediately." Martha smiled reminiscently. "It was the start of an enduring friendship."

They talked for hours. Martha told Sabena details of her long association with Katherine Fabian, then provided background information on each of the family members. It was late when Sabena finally rose to leave.

"Do you really think you can find Lucky?" Martha asked at the door.

"I have a few ideas," Sabena replied noncommittally. "Let's see what I turn up tonight."

Martha looked at her doubtfully. "I honestly think you should concentrate on Katherine's relatives rather than on Jake."

"I intend to do both. You're probably right about him, but since an attorney-client relationship is privileged, his clients might have told him quite a lot."

"Even if they did, he wouldn't tell you."

"Not if he knew I was a private detective." Sabena grinned. "But Jake thinks he's taking a tourist out on a date."

Sabena dressed carefully that night, avoiding anything too obviously sexy. Her pleated navy skirt was short enough to show off her excellent legs, however, and the demure turtlenecked white sweater clung to her small, high breasts. With luck, Jake would be intrigued enough to let down his guard.

She kept her makeup simple, also. Fortunately, her thick black lashes didn't need mascara, and her cheeks were naturally pink. Perfume was the one thing she didn't skimp on. Even girls from Pear Blossom must wear perfume. After brushing her long black hair and letting it float casually around her shoulders, she slipped into a jacket.

Sabena's pulse rate speeded up when she got out of a cab in front of the McConnell gallery. Was it the usual adrenaline that pumped when she was on a case? Or did the prospect of seeing Jake again have something to do with it? Sabena dismissed the thought and went inside.

The large room was crowded with stylishly dressed men and women talking animatedly and sipping wine. No one seemed very interested in the paintings that lined the walls. As Sabena was glancing around, Jake came up to her.

"I was wondering how I'd find you in this crowd," she said. "Am I late?"

"No, I was a little early. I came directly from the office."

"You should have told me you had to work late. Now I feel guilty for asking you to come tonight."

"Don't feel guilty." He smiled. "I've been looking forward to this all day."

Sabena gazed up at him with limpid blue eyes. "So have I."

"I must admit I've never heard of Kleinhoff before, but I like his work. Where have you seen it?"

"I haven't." It would have been foolish to lie when she could be tripped up so easily. "I just wanted to see what a gallery show was like."

"I'm crushed," he said mockingly. "I'd hoped perhaps *I* was the attraction."

"I'm sure you get more than your share of female admiration," Sabena answered.

"Appearances can be deceiving."

"That's true," she replied demurely.

"Take your case." His voice was casual. "If I didn't know better, I'd say you were a New Yorker."

"Why would you think that?"

His eyes flicked over her in a glance that held equal parts of appreciation and thoughtfulness. "I don't know exactly. Perhaps it's a certain air of self-assurance."

"Women who live in New York aren't the only ones who have confidence," she objected.

"You're right, of course."

Jake was being deceptively docile. What did he suspect her of? He couldn't have guessed the truth. Or could he? Sabena decided some damage control was in order.

"This isn't my first visit to New York," she said. "Maybe some of the sophistication rubbed off on me."

"How often do you get here?"

"Whenever I can. There's so much to do—the museums, music, Broadway. I adore the theater, don't you?"

Her hope of distracting him failed. "If you visit New York often, it's strange that you never met Katherine Fabian."

"I didn't like to intrude. Martha and I met for lunch, instead. Do you want to know what restaurants we went to?" she asked ironically.

His smile held the same irony. "Not unless you want to tell me. You seem rather defensive. Why would that be?"

"If I am, it's because I'm not used to being cross-examined." She chose a direct approach. "Why are you so interested in me?"

"I thought we'd established that."

"Not to my satisfaction. Since we're on opposite sides of the fence, it seems strange that you'd be consorting with the enemy."

"I don't consider you *or* Martha an enemy. My relationship with the Fabian family is purely business."

"It's a dirty job, but somebody has to do it?" Sabena asked derisively.

"You must admit that Miss Fabian's will was rather eccentric."

"Perhaps, but it was *her* money. People should be entitled to do what they want with their estates."

"*If* they're of sound mind. Anyone who leaves millions of dollars to a cat is either senile or outright crazy."

"Not necessarily, and she only left it to him for his lifetime. Your clients don't even need the money. They're simply greedy."

"Everyone needs money. Have you ever tried living without it?"

"No, and I don't imagine you have, either," she answered tartly.

Jake's elegant suit was either a Brioni or an Armani, and the thin gold watch on his wrist had cost a fortune. It was obvious that he was materialistic. No wonder he didn't understand things like devotion and concern for an animal.

"Do you always make snap judgments about people?" he asked with a raised eyebrow.

"Didn't you form an instant opinion of *me*?" she countered.

"No, I'm still trying to figure you out."

As they were staring warily at each other, oblivious to the rest of the people in the crowded room, someone jostled Sabena from behind. She was pushed forward into Jake. His arms closed to steady her, and for one disturbing moment their bodies joined.

Sabena was made vividly aware of something she'd already suspected. Jake's broad shoulders were his own, not due to padding. He had the lean, lithe body of an athlete in his prime. When his taut thighs brushed against hers and the clean male scent of his skin filled her nostrils, Sabena's breath caught in her throat.

She moved away self-consciously. Avoiding his eyes, she touched his collar tentatively. "I'm afraid I got lipstick on you."

"Don't worry about it. Nobody will mind."

"That's the joy of being single," she said lightly.

"There are benefits," he agreed. "This place is a zoo. Shall we get out of here and go to dinner?"

Sabena was abruptly reminded of why she was there. "I guess we should take a look at the paintings first."

They worked their way over to the fringes of the crowd where colorful paintings lined the walls. Sabena's pulse rate gradually returned to normal as they inspected the vivid canvases, although she was still very aware of Jake's nearness. Every now and then she glanced around for Emily, and finally her vigil was rewarded.

"Oh look, there's Emily," she said. "Is that her fiancé?"

Emily was talking to a handsome young blond man. He wasn't Sabena's type. His features were a little too perfect, and his clothes were too trendy. He was the ultimate yuppie, but she could see why some women would find him attractive.

Jake followed the direction of her gaze. "Yes, that's Don. Let's go before they see us."

"You don't like Emily and Don?" Sabena watched for his reaction.

"I heartily approve of both of them—during working hours. I'm on my own time now."

"That sounds very cold," she protested. "Don't you feel a rapport with your clients?"

"They're paying for my expertise, not my friendship."

"You're a very cynical man," Sabena said slowly.

"It's a cruel world out there. Survival of the fittest isn't merely a cliché."

As she gazed at his hawklike face, Sabena felt a slight chill. Jake would do anything necessary to get what he wanted, and he had the means. She wouldn't care to be the one who stood in his way.

"You can't let—" He broke off to smother a groan. "Too late. They're coming over."

"Hi, Jake." Emily reached them, followed by her fiancé. "I didn't know you two would be here tonight."

Jake's charming manner gave no indication of his true feelings. "I'm surprised we were lucky enough to bump into each other in this crowd." He introduced Sabena to Don Scudder.

The blond man's admiration was more abundant than she thought necessary. "Jake certainly has an eye for beautiful women," he told Sabena.

"You do, too," Jake reminded him.

"We're both fortunate," Don answered smoothly.

"Isn't this fun?" Emily asked. "It's such a nice turnout. Kleinhoff is going to be a major artist someday."

"I wish him luck, but personally, I came for the wine and cheese," Don said.

"You don't mean that," she said indulgently.

"Emily is the idealist of this couple," Don told them. "I'm the practical one who takes advantages of all the perks."

"I'm not sure a free glass of wine is worth it," Jake remarked. "Unless you happen to like crowds of strangers."

"Strangers are merely people you haven't met yet," Don answered in all seriousness. "We could both make valuable contacts here."

"Lawyers aren't supposed to solicit clients," Jake said sardonically. "It's called ambulance chasing."

"That's stupid," Don stated. "You have to take advantage of every opportunity that comes your way. Who cares what labels people put on you?"

"With an attitude like that, I could get disbarred."

"Not you, Jake. You're too smart for that. Look what you're doing for my girl here and her family. I like a man who goes for the jugular."

Emily glanced at Sabena, then away again, looking uncomfortable. She tried to change the subject. "Did anything interesting happen after I left today? I wouldn't have gone if I'd known the reason, but it was worth it to get Aunt Katherine's locket."

"I'm surprised that old bat, Martha, didn't make off with the whole lot." Don scowled. "There's a healthy market for antique jewelry, even without precious stones."

"Sabena is a friend of Martha's," Emily told him swiftly.

Don turned his attention on Sabena, without approval this time. "Don't expect me to apologize. That woman is trying to cheat Emily out of her inheritance."

"You're out of line, Don," Jake told him authoritatively.

"I have a right to say what I think." The blond man's temper flared at being challenged.

"This is neither the time nor the place."

"I wasn't aware that I needed your permission," Don drawled. "Aren't you forgetting who's paying you?"

"Not you." Jake's voice was quiet, but the steely look on his face made the other man uneasy.

Don's eyes shifted. "I have Emily's interests at heart."

"I'm sure you do," Jake answered impassively. He turned to Emily. "Sabena and I were just leaving. It was nice seeing you."

"Yes, you too," she replied, looking troubled.

When they were outside, Jake hailed a cab. "I thought we'd go to the Rainbow Room, if that's all right with you."

"It sounds lovely," Sabena answered absently. Was Jake annoyed at Don because he was a jerk—or because he talked too much? Were the Fabians paying for more than legal advice?

"I'm sorry about that unpleasantness," Jake said in the taxi. "Don is a bit of a hothead."

"It's funny that he's more hostile toward Martha than Emily is. Unless she's simply better at hiding her feelings."

"No, I think Emily is genuinely fond of Martha. She's known her for most of her life."

"But she hasn't spoken up in support of her. Even Don thinks that Martha is up to something shady."

"It's understandable that he would be protective of Emily's interests."

"I suppose so," Sabena admitted. "When do they plan to get married?"

"I don't believe they've set a date yet."

"A young couple just starting out could really use Emily's share of the money," Sabena mused. "I don't imagine a junior curator's job pays a great deal."

"You're probably right," Jake answered neutrally.

"But Don is a stockbroker. It seems to me they could afford to get married on his salary alone."

Jake's expression was unreadable in the dimness of the taxi. "Do you always try to solve the problems of people you've just met?"

"I like Emily," Sabena explained carefully. "She was the only one who realized Martha might like something personal of Katherine's."

"Yes, that was thoughtful of her."

"Of course the jewelry wasn't worth a great deal."

"Weren't you the one who prized sentiment so highly?" he asked mockingly. "Why question Emily's good deed?"

"You're right. I was thinking of the amount she stands to gain if the will is declared invalid, but it wasn't very generous-spirited of me. I guess the size of the estate clouded my judgment."

"You're not the only one who's been guilty of that crime," Jake said evenly.

Did he have someone specific in mind? Or was he speaking from personal experience? Which side of the law was Jake really on?

"Would you commit a crime for a million dollars?" she asked offhandedly.

"That's too broad a question. I'd have to know the circumstances, and what kind of crime we're talking about."

"You just flunked the quiz," she told him with a slight laugh. "Any kind of crime should be off-limits."

"If we're speaking theoretically. In the real world, anybody is capable of breaking the law, given suitable provocation or incentive." Jake's expression was unfathomable.

"I can't agree with you. A normal person knows the difference between right and wrong."

"Dear little Sabena, you *are* an innocent, after all," he said, chuckling. "Do you honestly think that would deter someone if the inducement was great enough?"

"Maybe not, but let's say the crime involved money. What if the person didn't really need it?"

"I see we're still talking about the will." Jake sighed in resignation.

"We might as well. It's on both our minds."

"I wouldn't say that," he murmured with a smile.

Sabena didn't allow herself to be distracted. "Suppose this person had a spotless reputation and enjoyed an upscale life-style. I realize nobody has all the things they might want, but let's say he has more than his share. Or her share," she added hastily. "Are you telling me that person would step over the line to get more?"

"You're obviously referring to Don, and I can't answer for him."

Did Jake honestly think she was talking about Don? It was clever of him to pretend she couldn't possibly mean himself. The taxi pulled over to the curb before she could try to pin him down.

Their discussion was cut short as a high-speed elevator whisked them to the top of Rockefeller Center where the magnificent view would have distracted anyone. Wide glass windows looked out over a fairy-tale city lit by thousands of sparkling lights in every jewel color.

The bar was crowded with people waiting for tables in the dignified dining room beyond. Sabena didn't know what magic Jake worked, but after he spoke to the maître d', they were shown to a choice table by the dance floor.

"I'm not really dressed for someplace this fancy." She frowned slightly. "I should have said so when you suggested it."

"Your mind was on other things," he said with a hint of mockery. "But I wouldn't worry about it. You look charming."

"You're just being polite. We both know a skirt and sweater aren't proper attire for the Rainbow Room."

"I don't know of a woman who looks better in them." His gaze moved appreciatively over what he could see of her slender body.

Although his compliment was conventional, Sabena had the uncomfortable feeling that he was accurately picturing her without the sweater. Jake must have undressed many women in his life. Was that what he had planned for her? She could almost feel his hands sliding under the hem of her sweater, smoothing her bare skin.

As a tide of warmth engulfed Sabena, she moistened her dry lips. The waiter's arrival couldn't have been more timely. After they'd ordered, Jake asked her to dance.

She moved into his arms with some trepidation. No man had ever had this effect on her, and she'd known quite a few. It was an effort to remember that he might not be what he seemed. And even if he was, Jake represented a threat to her client.

Sabena reviewed the list of reasons to steer clear of him. But when he drew her close, conscious thought ceased. She relaxed in his arms, letting him mold her soft curves to his hard frame.

Jake was an excellent dancer, as she'd suspected he would be. Did he excel at everything? Didn't he have a single flaw? She slid her hand over his muscular shoulder. No physical ones, anyway.

Jake's lips brushed her temple. "How do I tell you that you feel like a cloud in my arms, without sounding like a high school boy?"

She tilted her head to gaze up at him. "Don't worry, no one would ever mistake you for one."

He smiled. "That's good, isn't it?"

"Depending on your behavior as an adult," she answered demurely.

"My intentions are strictly honorable. I'd like to make love to you."

"You call that honorable?" she demanded.

"*I'd* consider it an honor." He grinned.

Sabena relaxed. "For a moment I thought you were serious."

"I am." His hand curled around her neck, and one long forefinger gently stroked the soft skin behind her ear. "I never joke about making love to a beautiful woman."

"We scarcely know each other," she said reprovingly.

"Can you think of a better way to get acquainted?" he asked in a deep velvet voice.

"Several," she replied stiffly.

"Ah, well, I'm a patient man."

"What makes you think that will get you anywhere?"

"A man can only hope." He kissed the tip of her nose.

Sabena suddenly realized he was teasing her. She felt foolish for overreacting. "I'm sure someone else will come along to console you if I'm a disappointment." She kept her voice airy to show that she knew he was joking.

Jake's amusement fled as he traced the shape of her mouth. "You could never be a disappointment."

"My experience can't compare to yours," she murmured.

"You don't need any." He smoothed the hair away from her face. "My greatest pleasure would be to bring you fulfillment."

Sabena was caught in his brilliant gaze like a doe in bright headlights. She could visualize everything Jake was promising. He would use his expertise to transport her to realms she'd never reached before, and then he'd cradle her in his arms as they floated down together from heaven.

The music stopped and he released her, breaking the spell. Sabena moved away from him wordlessly, averting her eyes.

Jake put his arms around her shoulders and led her back to their table. "You needn't worry, honey, I'm harmless."

She forced a smile. "You don't honestly expect me to believe that?"

"I guarantee you, I've never forced myself on a lady."

He didn't have to, she thought. Jake would be the ultimate experience a woman could have with a man. She dismissed the notion determinedly. His prowess meant nothing to her. He wasn't even a friend!

Sabena's discomfort vanished during dinner. Jake exerted himself to be charming, and his efforts would have disarmed women a lot less vulnerable than Sabena. She was having such a good time that her conscience began to trouble her. This wasn't supposed to be a date. She made an effort to guide Jake back to the case.

"I'm glad we went tonight, but a gallery reception isn't anything like a museum show," she remarked.

"No, it's more of a social event. If you like crowds and a lot of noise," he added wryly.

"I thought it was great fun—except for that slight unpleasantness with Don. He's a very angry young man."

"Wouldn't you be if someone stood between you and a million dollars?" Jake asked sardonically.

"Are you implying he's marrying Emily for her money?"

"Not at all," Jake answered quickly. "I have no reason to believe they aren't deeply in love."

"I suppose you would know."

The skepticism in her voice wasn't lost on him. "You don't seem to approve of Don. Most women find him quite personable."

"He's nice-looking, but he has an abrasive personality."

"Don is a typical yuppie," Jake said with thinly veiled contempt. "He expects everything in life to be easy. He doesn't know the meaning of adversity."

"Are you implying that *you* do?" Sabena couldn't quite hide her derision.

"I don't know why, but you've formed an erroneous opinion of me. Contrary to what you think, I'm not part of the trust fund and inheritance crowd. I've worked hard to get where I am. In a way, I understand Don's frustration. Katherine Fabian's will is absurd."

"From what I've seen of her relatives, that cat is more deserving of the money than they are," Sabena replied tartly.

"You have a very cavalier attitude toward money. I'm glad life has been so good to you."

"Aren't you the one who's jumping to conclusions now?"

"I'm correct, am I not? You haven't taken any really hard knocks."

"I suppose not," she admitted grudgingly. "But that's just a lucky guess."

"Not really. It's my business to read people. I can tell the ones who never had to claw their way up. They lack the killer instinct."

Suddenly Sabena got a glimpse of the real man under all the charm and sophistication. Jake's eyes were more green than gold now. He was a predator who would show no mercy.

"Was...your early life...hard?" she faltered.

"You might say that. My father died when I was twelve, leaving my mother with three children to support. It was a struggle to put enough food on the table, but we survived. We all worked, and nobody ever gave us anything. So you'll have to excuse me for not getting sentimental over a cat."

"Did you get a scholarship to college?"

"No, I worked my way through. Scholarships come tied up in red tape. I didn't want anyone to own me."

"You don't trust anybody, do you?" Sabena asked slowly.

"I'll tell you something I've learned. When it really counts, you're out there all alone." His hard face relaxed in a charming smile. "Now you know the story of my life. From rags to riches—or at least, relative comfort."

"More than that, from the way Harriet was complaining about your fee."

He chuckled. "You've seen that commercial on television? I'm worth it."

"I don't doubt that for a moment." She slanted a glance at him. "Do you think you'll be able to break the will?"

"We'll have to wait and see, won't we?"

"Are you going to claim Lucky crawled away somewhere to die of natural causes?" Sabena asked. "That's the only way your clients can collect."

"I'm beginning to think you're more interested in the case than you are in me," he answered lightly. "Is that why you're here tonight?"

"You know better than that," she protested. "I was intrigued by you from the moment we met." That part wasn't a lie.

"I didn't know I'd made an impression. This could be the start of a beautiful friendship."

"A short one. I'm only visiting, remember?"

"You said you'd be here for a couple of weeks. We could get to know each other extremely well before you leave." His voice was like liquid honey.

"I don't go in for brief encounters," she answered primly.

Jake smiled. "Haven't you ever heard of quality time?"

"Not used in that context."

"When a man and a woman are attracted to each other, doesn't it make sense to seize the moment?" He tucked a strand of silky hair behind her ear before trailing his fingers down her neck.

She twitched away nervously. "You're presuming a lot from one small compliment."

"You *don't* find me attractive? Then I can only conclude that my suspicion was correct. You're just here tonight to get information out of me."

"That's ridiculous!" Jake was too astute for comfort. "You know perfectly well that you're a very charming man."

"You aren't merely saying that?"

"Certainly not! Any woman would be thrilled to be with you." In her rush to allay his suspicions, Sabena had overdone it.

"Then what are we waiting for? Let's go to my apartment. I'll get the check."

"No! I . . . you're rushing me."

"I'm sorry, honey. You're not finished with your coffee. Never mind, we'll have another cup at my place." A little smile tilted his firm mouth. "You're worth waiting for."

"I'm not going to your apartment."

Sabena's mind boggled at the thought. If Jake was this enticing here in a public restaurant, imagine what would happen when they were alone! He had potent ways of convincing a woman.

"You'd rather go to your place?" he asked. "That's all right, too, although the thought of you in my bed is irresistible."

She drew a deep breath. "I am not going to sleep with you."

"I don't expect to get much sleep, either," he teased.

"How can I get through to you?" she exclaimed in frustration. "I scarcely know you, and even if I did, I still wouldn't go to bed with you. This is all there is. I'm sorry if I wasted your evening."

"It wasn't wasted. I think I got more out of it than you did."

"You aren't annoyed?" she asked uncertainly.

"Not in the slightest. I never expected to spend the night with you," he answered calmly.

"You mean it was all a joke?" she asked with dawning indignation. "You just wanted to get a rise out of me?"

"Not entirely. I would have been surprised and delighted if you'd taken me up on my offer. You're a very desirable woman. Much too beautiful to play dangerous games." His voice held a flinty note.

"I don't know what you're talking about."

"It's unwise to lead men on. You could be extremely sorry," he said softly.

"I'm not responsible if you got the wrong idea." Sabena's bluster covered quivering nerves. She was right about Jake. He *was* ruthless.

He reverted disconcertingly to his former charm. "Perhaps you're right. You fit in so well in the big city that I'd forgotten you were a little country girl."

"I've never met a man like you," she murmured, which was the truth.

He smiled. "Are we still friends?"

"I hope so. I wouldn't want you for an enemy," she said frankly.

"I could never be your enemy, Sabena." Pinpoints of light glittered in his eyes as they ranged over her delicate features. "I may think you're misguided, and I might have to take steps that you think are harsh, but I'll try not to hurt you."

What was he really saying? That he intended to break the will and put Martha out? No, that's what he'd been hired to do. She already knew that. How could he hurt her, Sabena wondered? There was no way. Still, an icy finger of fear touched her spine.

Chapter Three

Jake couldn't have been a more delightful companion during the rest of the evening. Sabena almost thought she'd imagined his veiled warning. Almost. Jake wasn't a man you got careless with.

They had more coffee and marvelous pastries from the dessert cart, and he told her amusing stories about some of his clients—omitting their names, naturally. She reluctantly brought the conversation back to the Fabians.

"What funny stories are you going to tell about your present clients?"

Jake shook his head. "Ethically, I can't discuss them with you."

"I don't expect you to give away your strategy or anything like that. I was referring to their personalities. They're all so eccentric, in various ways."

"Why are you interested in them?"

"Just curiosity about the idle rich. I presume they *are* all rich?" she asked casually.

"In varying degrees."

Sabena wasn't deterred by Jake's guarded answer. "Marguerite must spend a fortune on clothes. That suit she had on today was a Chanel. And Martha described Charles as something of a roué. That life-style must be expensive. Harriet is the only one who doesn't seem to throw her money around. Because she can't afford to?"

"It's never wise to count someone else's money, but I suspect Harriet could pay off a good portion of the national debt," Jake said wryly.

"She doesn't seem to get much pleasure out of her wealth."

He shrugged. "Everything is relative. Some people enjoy hoarding."

"I never could understand that."

"What would *you* do if you suddenly came into a windfall?" He watched her with an unreadable expression.

Sabena pondered for a moment. "Pay off my bills, maybe buy something extravagant like a cashmere sweater, and put the rest in the bank. There isn't anything I really yearn for."

"So you don't really need the money, either."

"The Fabian money? What does that have to do with me? I thought you were speaking in generalities."

"I was." Jake stood and held out his hand to her. "Let's dance. I'm heartily sick of the Fabians, and dancing is the only way you'll let me hold you in my arms."

The need to guard her emotions was wearing. All of Sabena's instincts warned her against Jake. But they were hard to follow when he held her close and seduced her in subtle ways—brushing his lips lightly across her forehead, caressing her back in a chaste, but sensual manner.

It was distracting, especially when she was trying to outwit him. How could she keep her mind on the Fabians? Sabena was almost glad when he mentioned an early-morning appointment.

"I have to get up early, too," she said without thinking.

"I thought you were on vacation."

"I am, but I don't want to spend it in bed."

Jake smiled. "I'm beginning to think you say provocative things like that on purpose."

"I was merely stating a fact. *You're* the one who insists on getting personal."

"You can't blame a guy for trying." He grinned.

"I really enjoyed tonight, Jake. Thank you for a lovely evening," she said as they walked outside and he flagged down a taxi.

"I did, too." He opened the cab door. "What's your address?"

"You don't have to take me home."

"Maybe not, but I intend to."

"We probably go in different directions. Where do you live?" she asked.

"On Seventieth, near Park."

"You see? I was right," she said triumphantly. "I live on Forty-fifth."

"You want a cab, or were you just waving your arm to ward off bats?" the driver asked irately.

"Get in," Jake ordered.

Sabena had to comply, although she would have preferred to keep her address a secret. Not that it really mattered. Her cover story would hold up.

When they reached her apartment building, Jake insisted on seeing Sabena to her door, over her protests.

"You don't have to treat me like a child," she declared.

"I can't seem to satisfy you," he answered dryly. "You're equally displeased when I notice you're a woman."

"I was only trying to be thoughtful. You said you have to get up early."

"I can spare a few moments for good manners."

He took the key out of Sabena's hand and opened the door. As she prepared to say a firm good-night, he looked over her shoulder.

"Your friend has a very tasteful apartment," he commented.

"It's small, but I think she's done nice things to it." Sabena was proud of the eclectic mix of antiques she'd found in secondhand shops.

"I like that coromandel screen. Nineteenth century?" Before she could think of a way to stop him, Jake had entered the living room.

Sabena followed reluctantly. "Yes, I believe it is."

He wandered around the room, examining a millefiori paperweight, an art deco vase. When he passed by a monogrammed pillow on the couch, she held her breath, hoping he wouldn't notice it. The hope was in vain.

"S.M. Aren't those your initials?" he asked.

"They're hers, too. Sally Monroe. That's how we happened to meet. Our seats in high school English class were assigned alphabetically. We've been friends ever since." Was she talking too much? Acting defensive? She couldn't judge Jake's reaction.

"Too bad she isn't here for your visit," he remarked casually.

"We were both disappointed, but I'd already bought my airline ticket and it was nonrefundable."

"Sally's loss is my gain. Maybe you'll have more time for me."

"It's entirely possible." She gazed up at him from under long lashes.

Suddenly the telephone rang. Sabena was so startled that she froze. While she hesitated, the answering machine clicked on.

"Hi, it's Pete. Sorry to call you so late, but something just came up. I might have a job for you if you're interested. Call me first thing in the morning."

That would be Peter Pulanski, a fellow private eye. He sometimes threw work her way if he had more than he could handle. Sabena reviewed the brief message, then breathed a little easier. The call could be explained away.

Jake was watching her without expression. "You're planning to move to New York?"

"Heavens no! That message was for Sally. She's a free-lance accountant. Too bad she missed out on a job."

"She already has one that keeps her hopping," he commented.

"That's true. Well...you have to get up early." Sabena tried to sound casual, although she couldn't wait to get him out of the apartment. Before something else happened.

"I don't want to leave, but I'd better." A little smile lurked around his firm mouth. "How about dinner and the theater tomorrow night?"

"That sounds wonderful."

Sabena's mind continued to work furiously after Jake left. Why had he asked her out again? It would be flattering to think he was really attracted to her, but too many things disproved that theory. Jake didn't trust her any more than she trusted him. Did he want to maintain contact for the same reason she did? Sabena couldn't help feeling a nagging little sense of disappointment.

The next morning Sabena dressed in jeans, a T-shirt and windbreaker, and running shoes. With very little makeup and her long hair caught back with a clip, she looked like a fresh-faced college student.

Her destination was Marguerite's apartment on Eighty-first Street. Martha had provided Sabena with the addresses of all the family.

A uniformed doorman stood in front of the elegant building, watching the traffic with a bored expression.

Sabena approached him, smiling bewitchingly. "Hi, isn't it a glorious day?"

His expression warmed as he gazed at her slender figure, accentuated by the tight jeans. "It would be if I didn't have to work."

"I know what you mean. Wouldn't it be nice if we could all be on a perpetual vacation?"

"Yeah, but the only way that's going to happen is if I win the lottery, or somebody dies and leaves me a fortune."

"Maybe one of your rich tenants will remember you in his will," she said casually.

"Fat chance! We got one woman here whose sister left all her money to her cat."

Sabena had struck pay dirt more easily than she'd expected. "It sounds like the sisters didn't get along," she remarked.

He shrugged. "Who knows? Must have been a weirdo, if you ask me."

Sabena grinned. "I guess your tenant wants to kick every cat she sees."

"I wouldn't blame her."

"Well, I guess *she* isn't a good prospect. I run a pet service—walking dogs and taking care of cats when the owners are on vacation. I'm looking for new clients."

"You've come to the wrong place. Animals aren't allowed in this building."

"Too bad." She slanted a glance at him. "I suppose you'd know if anybody was keeping one secretly."

He chuckled. "You're wasting your time. Nothing goes on around here that I don't know about."

After a little more conversation, Sabena left, convinced that the doorman was telling the truth. He probably did have inside information on all the tenants. Not that Marguerite was absolved—it was just too much to hope she was hiding Lucky in her own apartment. That was simply one place to cross off the list.

Sabena's next stop was Harriet's apartment house, a few blocks from Marguerite's. She intended to use the same M.O. with the doorman, but as she approached, a woman came out of the building and stopped to talk to him. Obviously not one of the tenants, she was wearing her coat over a white uniform.

Sabena knelt down and tied her shoe while she waited for the woman to leave. The two chatted for a few moments, taking no notice of her.

After exchanging comments on the weather, the doorman asked, "Where are you off to this early in the morning?"

"The grocery store—and not a minute too soon. I'm telling you, that woman would try the patience of a saint!"

He chuckled. "Mrs. Sheridan isn't easy to get along with. You're the third housekeeper she's had this year."

"I'll bet they carted the others off to the loony bin. She's after me all day long. Why do you have to use so much soap? Don't throw out those crusts of bread, we can make croutons out of them. I don't know how much longer I can take it."

"Life is hard," he said sympathetically.

"Tell me! Well, I better get a move on. If she thinks I enjoyed myself for a few minutes, she'll make me work overtime."

"Take it easy, Bessie," the doorman called as she walked away.

Sabena followed at a discreet distance. Her plans underwent a change as soon as she found out the woman worked for Harriet.

When they reached the market, Sabena took a basket and filled it with a random assortment of cans and packages, keeping an eye on Bessie. As soon as they neared the pet food section, Sabena walked past her, then stopped and scanned the shelves, positioning her cart so it blocked the aisle.

In a few moments, the housekeeper caught up with her. "Can I get by?" she asked.

"Oh, I'm sorry." Sabena moved the cart, saying, "I was trying to decide what cat food to buy. They have so many different brands that it's confusing."

"This is the kind *we* use." Bessie pointed at the shelf. "They're all pretty much alike, and this one's the cheapest."

That would appeal to Harriet. Sabena concealed her surge of excitement. "What kind of cat do you have?"

"He's just a stray alley cat that turned up out of nowhere."

"That's how I got mine. Don't tell me yours is black, too?"

"No, he's gray and white. Frankly, I could do without all that long cat hair on the furniture, but my kids are crazy about him."

Well, there went *that* lead, Sabena thought. Lucky was short-haired, besides being solid black. It didn't put Harriet in the clear, however.

"You have to love cats," she persisted. "Although, I don't know anybody who doesn't."

"You haven't met the woman I work for."

"People surprise you. I'll bet she'd take in a stray."

"Guess again. That woman's too stingy to feed a canary," Bessie said succinctly.

That meant if Harriet was harboring Lucky, she was keeping him somewhere other than in her apartment. A cat wasn't something she could hide from her housekeeper. After a few more words, Sabena moved away.

Charles Fabian was next on her list, but first she checked in with her answering service. There were a couple of messages concerning a job she'd just completed, requiring some time-consuming follow-up work. This took up the rest of the day. She returned home with just enough time to change for her date that evening.

The telephone rang as she unlocked the door. It was Jake. "I'll be stuck here at the office for another hour," he told her. "So I was wondering if you'd mind having dinner after the theater instead of before."

"I wouldn't mind a bit. In fact I'd prefer it," she answered. "I just got home myself. Why don't I meet you at the theater? Then you won't have to rush."

"That would take the pressure off," he admitted. "I can come directly from work."

Since she now had plenty of time, Sabena took a relaxing bubble bath, telling herself the anticipation she felt was because she was doing her job well. Jake was a promising source of information. If he was also stimulating company, that was simply a bonus.

The dress she chose was a sophisticated black sheath, very simple except for a wide jeweled belt that accentuated her small waist. For tonight at least, she dropped her country-girl pose. Even in small towns, women dressed up for a date.

They used makeup, too. Sabena subtly applied mascara and eye shadow, and then, not wishing to appear *too* sophisticated, merely brushed her long hair and let it float loosely around her shoulders.

Sabena arrived at the theater a few minutes before Jake. She watched him get out of a cab, noticing several other women watching him, as well. Jake looked handsome and vital, in spite of his long day. She had a moment to admire the easy coordination of his long-limbed body before he spotted her by the entrance.

He made his way through the crowd. "Have you been waiting long?"

"No, I just got here," she assured him.

His expression changed to admiration as he made a more comprehensive appraisal of her. "You look fantastic!"

"I'm glad you noticed." Sabena laughed. "I'd hate to think all that extra effort was wasted."

"You did this for me?"

Her eyes shifted away from his brilliant gaze. "A Broadway play is quite an event in my life."

"I hope the entire evening will be eventful," he said softly.

"Yes, well, hadn't we better go inside and find our seats?" she asked, feeling more like prey than predator.

Their seats were excellent, and the musical comedy merited the rave reviews it had received. Sabena thoroughly enjoyed the performance, but she remained conscious of Jake's presence, almost intimately close and unmistakably masculine.

Most of the theaters in the Broadway district let out at the same time. The resulting crush of humanity poured onto the sidewalks, vying for an inadequate number of taxis. Manners were forgotten as people jostled each other, regardless of gender.

Jake was undaunted by the odds. Guiding Sabena through the crowd, he snagged a cab almost miraculously.

"I don't know how you do it," she marveled as they drove away.

"I'm a native New Yorker."

"It has to be more than that. So were most of those people we left behind."

"They don't have the killer instinct." He grinned. " 'Show no mercy' is my motto."

Jake was only joking, but Sabena thought there was more than a grain of truth in his remark. People recognized that quality in him and proceeded with caution. It was something to think about.

She put aside her reservations during dinner at an elegant restaurant on the East Side. Jake was not only charming, he was interesting, as well. They talked about politics and movies, censorship and the state of the arts. Sabena had never met a man so intellectually stimulating. She completely forgot her reason for being with him.

Jake brought her down to earth while they were having coffee. They'd been talking about the rising cost of living in big cities. "Has Martha made plans to move out of the Fabian house?"

"Don't you think that's a little premature?" Sabena asked sharply.

"I didn't mean immediately, but surely she's considered the eventuality."

"Not concerning the near future. Martha thinks Lucky will turn up."

"Do you share that belief?"

"Anything is possible," Sabena answered evasively. "He could have wandered off to look for Katherine. He must miss her a lot."

"Is that the reason for the bogus cat? Martha thinks the real one will return?"

"You believe she replaced Lucky to keep her job, but you're wrong."

Jake gazed at her enigmatically. "Even if Martha didn't make the substitution, she was almost certainly aware of it. Cats have personalities like people. Wouldn't you notice a change in an animal you'd seen every day for a number of years?"

"Maybe she thought he'd been affected by Katherine's death."

"Maybe," he repeated skeptically.

"Martha is getting a bad rap. She doesn't even *want* to stay on, now that Katherine is gone."

Jake wasn't impressed. "If you say so. But not many people would consider it a hardship to live rent-free in a mansion on Park Avenue."

"Including your clients."

"The difference is, they're the rightful heirs."

"It isn't right to abduct and kill a cat," Sabena replied heatedly.

"Do you know something I don't?" His voice was deceptively mild.

"No, I think *you're* the one with the answers. How can you represent people who would do such a rotten thing?"

"Everyone is entitled to a lawyer. You've heard the line on television a hundred times. If you cannot afford an attorney, one will be provided for you. People who can afford to pay deserve the same privilege."

"So you admit that one of your clients did away with Lucky!"

"Not at all. I was merely reminding you of basic civil rights."

"How about Martha's civil rights? She's been accused unfairly."

"I wouldn't say she'd actually been accused of anything," Jake said carefully.

"You heard the things Harriet said about her at the Fabian house the other day."

A look of annoyance passed over his strong face. "Harriet is a difficult woman. She gives everyone a hard time."

"That's no excuse. She's a thoroughly disagreeable old tyrant. I'm sure she wouldn't think twice about wringing a defenseless cat's neck."

He smiled at her vehemence. "I doubt if even Harriet would be that self-indulgent. Not when it would cost her a fortune."

Sabena slanted a glance at him. "Will the heirs sell the house if the court rules in their favor?"

"I imagine that would be the only solution. The property is worth a great deal of money, and none of them could afford to reimburse the others for their share." His expression was bland as he added, "But since you say Martha wants to move on, that shouldn't concern either of you."

"I was thinking about Greta and Lars. Losing their home is scary for older people."

"The money they were left should calm their fears."

Sabena gazed at the hard planes of his face. Jake's high cheekbones and square jaw could have graced a classic marble statue. He was just as remote and unfeeling, too. She lowered her lashes with a sense of defeat. What had made her think she could find a chink in this man's armor?

Jake put his hand over hers. It was large and capable, like everything else about him. "I'm not all bad," he said persuasively, as though he'd read her thoughts.

Ignoring the tingle that radiated from his touch, she answered, "You aren't Mr. Sensitivity, either."

"I'm a realist, honey. You have to be in our world today. The sentimentalists are the ones who get hurt."

"Not always. Anyway, it's worth the risk. You can't go through life without letting anyone get close to you."

"You've formed an erroneous opinion of me." His hand tightened.

"I doubt it." Sabena withdrew her own hand.

She was sure Jake had let many women get close to him in a physical sense, but she suspected he'd never given anything but his body. He would make love the way he did everything else, superbly, and his partners would never know the difference. It was sad, though. The man under all those layers of reserve must be fascinating.

"It's getting late," she remarked, suppressing a sigh. "Do you plan to get up early again?"

"No, but you must be tired. You've had a long day."

"Don't worry about me. I'm used to it."

"Do you always work this hard?"

He smiled. "It's a hard habit to break."

"What you need is a vacation."

He shook his head. "I'd spend the entire time calling the office to check on my cases."

"It's a good thing you aren't married."

"You're right. I'd make a lousy husband." He signaled for the check.

Sabena looked at him curiously. "I realize you're not at a loss for female companionship, but haven't you ever wanted to have children?"

"I'd probably be a rotten father, too," he answered indirectly.

The waiter arrived with the check, preventing her from pursuing the subject.

Sabena felt uncharacteristically nervous when Jake walked her to the door of her apartment. She'd wondered before if a date was going to kiss her good-night, but never with such mixed emotions. She had an uneasy feeling that a kiss from Jake wouldn't be soon forgotten.

"Thank you for a lovely evening." She smiled tentatively. "I really enjoyed it."

"So did I. You're interesting to talk to."

"I try to stay reasonably well-informed."

"That's admirable," he answered absently. His eyes wandered over her classic features, then lingered on her generous mouth. "You're also amazingly beautiful."

"That's quite a compliment, coming from a connoisseur of women."

Sabena's voice trembled slightly, in spite of her effort to keep her tone light. Jake's intense scrutiny was bad enough, but when he cupped her cheek in his palm and ran his thumb slowly over her bottom lip, she felt terribly vulnerable.

"You aren't like any other woman I've ever met," he murmured, curving one arm around her waist and drawing her closer.

Sabena was transfixed by the golden glow in his eyes. She had to fight against the urge to wind her arms around his neck and let her taut body relax in his embrace.

Managing a breathless laugh, she said, "I expected something more original from you."

"What do you want to hear? That you're like a lovely wood nymph with eyes the color of a mountain lake?" His fingers trailed down her neck.

"That's more poetic, at least." She moistened her dry lips, which was a mistake. His attention focused on them again.

"You inspire poetry." He kissed the corner of her mouth, a tantalizing little caress that made her want more. "You're a bewitching mixture of innocence and guile." One hand tangled in her long hair, tugging her head back so he could kiss the hollow in her throat where a pulse beat wildly.

Sabena knew it was time to call a halt, but the words wouldn't come out. Jake had an almost hypnotic power over her. There had been an undeniable chemistry between them from the moment they'd met, and it became more volatile with each subsequent meeting.

"Sweet little Sabena." His lips slid up her neck.

Fighting for control of the situation, she said haltingly, "Well . . . I guess I'd better go in now."

He framed her face between his palms and stared at her with conflicting emotions. "I think that's a very good idea."

Neither moved, however. Then Jake slowly closed the small distance between them. Sabena continued to stare into his brilliant eyes until his lips touched hers. Then her lashes fluttered down.

Jake's kiss was everything she thought it would be, dominantly male, yet gentle. He coaxed her lips apart and explored the sweetness inside, giving as much pleasure as he took. Any misgivings she might have had melted away in a spreading warmth that threatened to turn into a bonfire. She clasped her arms around his neck and pressed closely against him.

Jake dragged his mouth away and buried his face in her hair. "You're so enchanting," he groaned. "You could make a man lose his head completely."

"Would that be so terrible?" she whispered, sliding her hands inside his jacket.

He raised his head to stare down at her rapt face. The raw desire she saw in his eyes almost frightened her. She'd never witnessed passion quite that primitive.

At the involuntary little sound she made, his expression changed. Loosening his embrace, he kissed her chastely and said, "Good night, Sabena. It was a nice evening."

She watched uncomprehendingly as he walked down the hall without looking back. She didn't move until the sound of his footsteps had died away.

Finally she went inside, trying to make sense out of what had just happened. Jake wanted her as badly as she wanted him, so why had he left so abruptly?

Not that she was complaining. Now that her own hot tide of passion had receded somewhat, Sabena was appalled at how easily she was ready to capitulate. What made Jake so different from other men? She'd never let her emotions cloud her judgment before, and it scared her. Jake was even more formidable than she suspected. From now on, her guard would be up at all times.

Martha phoned early the next morning. "I don't suppose you have anything to report, or I would have heard from you," she said.

"I did some preliminary legwork, but it's only been two days," Sabena reminded her.

"I probably sent you on a wild-goose chase." Martha sighed.

"You mustn't get discouraged so easily. An investigation takes time."

"I'm afraid we don't have much time left. That's what I called to tell you. An appraiser came to the door yesterday. That means the Fabians expect a judgment in their favor."

"I never heard of the courts moving that fast. Who sent him?"

"I asked that question, but he was very evasive. I never really got an answer."

"I hope you didn't let him in!"

"Not without proper authorization. I'm not that naive. But I have a feeling he'll be back," Martha said hopelessly. "Someone was just trying to bypass the paperwork."

"They must have done it without Jake's knowledge. He's too careful to cut corners."

"Is he?"

Martha's cynical question echoed Sabena's own opinion. Jake would take chances if the stakes were high enough. Sabena forced herself to keep an open mind.

"Weren't you the one who said Jake couldn't be involved?" she asked.

"Not in the theft of Lucky, but naturally he'd push his advantage. Sending an appraiser without authorization is a rather minor infraction."

"I don't think you have to worry about imminent eviction," Sabena said. "Have you spoken to the executor of the estate?"

"It wouldn't do any good. Prescott, Goodbody and Mason is a dignified old law firm. They were appalled at all the publicity over Katherine's will. Mr. Lovejoy, the executor, just wants the notoriety to die down."

"Maybe you should hire your own attorney," Sabena suggested.

"That would only perpetuate the notion that I'm trying to stay on, no matter what it takes."

"Well, at least you can make the heirs wait for due process. That will give me more time to see what I can dig up."

"Do you have any leads at all?"

Sabena was reluctant to admit she didn't. "I found out that neither Harriet nor Marguerite are hiding Lucky in their apartments."

"So that only leaves Charles. And I suppose Emily," Martha added grudgingly.

"Not at all. Either of the sisters could have stashed Lucky somewhere else. It was really too much to hope that they'd be stupid enough to be keeping him in either of their apartments."

"How can you possibly find out where he is, then?"

Sabena had no idea at the moment, but she kept her voice confident. "That's what I do for a living. First I'm going to check out Charles, also Emily and her fiancé. Then I'll get back to Harriet and Marguerite."

"Don can't be involved," Martha objected. "He would only benefit indirectly, and then only after they were married. Engagements have been broken."

"I don't think this one will be," Sabena answered ironically. "Emily will be a very rich young woman some day. Anyway, everyone is a suspect at this point."

"Including Jake?"

"He's still on the list," Sabena said grimly.

"Did he say anything significant when you were with him?"

Sabena could think of several things, but they didn't necessarily pertain to the case. "Jake is very careful not to commit himself."

"I thought you'd be wasting your time."

"Even disciplined people slip up," Sabena argued.

"Good luck," Martha replied sarcastically.

"Well, my next target won't be as challenging. I plan to see Emily today."

"I'm sure you're wasting your time there, too. Emily is a nice girl. She isn't greedy like the rest of her family."

"You never really know about people."

"I've known her for years," Martha insisted. "She's always been thoughtful and kind. Lucky adored her. He followed her around like a dog."

"I rest my case," Sabena murmured.

"That doesn't prove anything. He liked most people. He just liked her more. I can't see Emily doing anything to harm him."

"You could be right, but you could also be wrong. I've seen murderers who looked like choirboys and were good to their mothers."

"Those were criminals!"

"We're talking about a criminal act," Sabena said patiently. "It's difficult to imagine anyone you know breaking the law, but it happens."

"I'll still wager it wasn't Emily."

Sabena laughed. "If I listened to you, my job would be a lot easier. So far you've eliminated five of my suspects—Emily and her fiancé, Jake, and the Swensons."

"You still suspect Greta and Lars."

"Let's just say I'd like to know if they start circling apartments for rent in the want ads."

"They don't know about the appraiser. I didn't want to worry them before it was necessary. The court will give us time to find another place to live, won't they?"

"I'm sure they will. But that's only a worst-case scenario. Let me get to work, and I'll call you as soon as I find out anything."

After she hung up, Sabena phoned Jake. She was put on hold for so long that she began to wonder if he was reluctant to talk to her. How could that be after his ardor last night? Jake was constantly confounding her.

Finally he came on the line. "Sorry to keep you waiting. What can I do for you, Sabena?" The words were polite, but his tone was businesslike.

His coolness made her more blunt than she intended to be. "Did you send a man out to appraise the Fabian house?"

"Why would I do that?" he countered.

"You tell *me*."

"Aren't you getting a little too involved in Martha's business?" he asked with a trace of irritation.

"She's concerned about being put out without notice. She's worried about the Swensons, too."

"That's nonsense," Jake said impatiently. "They'll all have ample time to find somewhere else to live."

"So you *have* started proceedings to evict them?"

"I can't talk to you about the case, Sabena." His tone was final.

"You talked about it last night."

"I did a lot of stupid things last night," he muttered.

"I'm sorry the evening was so unpleasant for you," she answered stiffly.

"I didn't say that." He paused to choose his words carefully. "You're a lovely lady and a charming companion. It's my own behavior I regret."

That was adding insult to injury! "I thought you were very entertaining," she said carelessly.

"I'm glad I didn't disappoint you." His voice sounded grim. "I was afraid you might have misunderstood some of my actions."

"I never gave them a second thought," she lied.

"Good. Was there anything else, Sabena? I have another call waiting." He was all business once more.

"No...I just wanted to find out about the appraiser," she faltered, feeling bruised by his indifference.

"I don't know anything about him, but I'll look into it."

Sabena replaced the receiver slowly. Why had Jake changed so drastically toward her? Had he only taken her out to find out if she knew anything, and then decided she didn't? That wouldn't explain the big seduction scene, even though he didn't follow through. An experienced man like Jake must have known he could have. Maybe even *he* had a conscience, Sabena thought bitterly.

Chapter Four

Sabena was hurt and angry after her conversation with Jake. She regretted the events of the previous evening more than he did, but at least *she'd* managed to be civil! No more, though. With any luck, this was the last time she'd ever have to speak to him.

Dismissing Jake firmly from her mind, Sabena went to her office and caught up on some paperwork until almost noon. When lunchtime approached, she went to the Metropolitan Museum.

A guard told her the administrative offices were located down a hallway from the main display rooms. Sabena wandered in that direction, then paused to examine a Corot painting. After a few moments, she drifted over to admire an exquisite sculpture by Gaston Lachaise. She seemed to be engrossed in the artwork, but her attention was actually focused on the entrance to the hall.

There was always a chance that Emily wouldn't go out to eat. But Sabena was betting that even if she'd brought her lunch, Emily would choose to take it outside on this glorious spring day.

Her hunch paid off after a long wait. A little after one o'clock, Emily came down the hall.

Sabena turned casually to look at another sculpture. Her face lit with mock surprise when she saw Emily. "I don't believe I actually bumped into somebody I know in this huge city!"

Emily smiled. "It isn't so strange. I work here."

"But it's such a big museum." Before Emily could wonder at the coincidence, also, Sabena hurried on. "You're so fortunate. What a fabulous place to work."

"Yes, I enjoy it."

"It must be wonderful to see all the special shows the rest of the country only reads about."

"Many of them travel to major cities."

"But not to small towns." Sabena smiled ruefully. "I practically live at the museums when I'm in New York City."

Emily gazed at her curiously. "Do you get here often? I don't recall Martha ever mentioning you."

Sabena repeated her story about not wanting to intrude on Katherine. "I wish now that I'd met her. She must have been quite special."

"Yes, Aunt Katherine was one of a kind." Emily glanced at her watch. "I'm afraid I have to go. I'm on my lunch hour."

"Would you mind terribly if I joined you?" Sabena looked at her appealingly. "I don't mind sight-seeing by myself, but I hate to eat alone."

"I don't think anyone enjoys it. I'd be happy to have company, but I'm only going to the deli around the corner. Nothing fancy," Emily warned.

"That suits me perfectly."

As they walked along the tree-lined street, Sabena decided to plunge right in. She wouldn't have unlimited time. "I'm sorry that Don was upset with me the other night."

"I'm the one who should apologize. It wasn't like him at all. Don is usually charming to everyone."

"I didn't take it personally. I realized he was angry at Martha, not me."

"This vendetta against Martha is so foolish!" Emily said impatiently. "She didn't influence Aunt Katherine."

"I agree with you, but the mix-up with the cats doesn't help her reputation."

Emily frowned. "I thought you were Martha's friend."

Sabena's expression was bland. "I am, but there's no point in ignoring what all of you are saying privately. Do *you* think Martha switched the cats?"

"I wouldn't know." Emily stared straight ahead.

"She certainly isn't the only one who could have. I'll bet you have some private suspicions of your own." Sabena watched for some sign that she'd hit a nerve.

Emily's only reaction was a definite coolness. "I haven't thought about it."

So much for the direct approach, Sabena thought. She set about mending fences. "I didn't know your aunt, but I can't say I approve of her will. It isn't fair to any of you."

Emily shrugged. "It was her money."

"But how could she leave it to a cat?"

"He meant a lot to her. Lucky was a very special cat."

"Martha told me he was very fond of you."

"The affection was mutual. You're right about one thing, though. Aunt Katherine should have realized she was creating an explosive situation. It's too bad Lucky had to suffer."

"You think he's dead?"

"I didn't say that," Emily replied swiftly. They reached an unprepossessing deli on a side street. "This is it, but you probably would prefer someplace nicer. You don't have to be polite."

Sabena refused to take the hint. "This looks just fine."

When they were seated at a small table with sandwiches and iced tea, Sabena took a different tack. "You have the best of all worlds, a good job in a great city, a handsome fiancé. When are you planning on getting married?"

"We haven't set a date yet." Emily smiled as she added, "Don would like it to be tomorrow."

"So you're the holdout," Sabena teased. "What are you waiting for?"

"I want to wait until all this turmoil is over. Aunt Harriet is forever calling family meetings, and Marguerite phones me every night with some new crisis. She's my grandmother, but she likes me to call her by her first name," Emily explained.

"I know. Martha told me."

"Our family is full of characters, I'm afraid, although Marguerite's pretensions are harmless. She simply refuses to grow old."

"I admire her spirit. She's still a very attractive woman."

"You wouldn't believe how many men she attracts." Emily grinned.

"All rich, I presume," Sabena commented. "They'd have to be to afford her. That suit she had on the other day was gorgeous."

"Yes, she likes the best of everything."

"I suppose she even has a country house to get away from it all."

"No, Marguerite prefers luxury hotels, preferably in Europe."

"There's nothing wrong with that. Keeping up two places must be a lot of work." Sabena was trying to find out if any of them owned vacation places where they could hide Lucky. "I suppose your aunt and uncle feel the same way."

"For different reasons. Aunt Harriet doesn't travel. She thinks anything past the East River is Indian territory. Uncle Charles is just the opposite. He's always on the go, but he finds it more economical to be a houseguest. He's visiting in the Hamptons right now."

So, wherever Lucky was, he wasn't sojourning in the country. All of Sabena's clues were negative ones so far. "Where do you and Don plan to live?" she asked.

"We haven't decided between his place and mine. Neither of them is really big enough, but the rent on anything larger is astronomical."

"It's too bad you can't take over Katherine's house," Sabena remarked artlessly. "Although, it's rather old-fashioned—all those carved mantelpieces and gilt wall sconces. I guess you'd prefer something more modern."

"Are you kidding? I'd kill for that house!" Emily's eyes were bright with animation. "Imagine having a real dining room and a garden you could putter around in on weekends. When I was a little girl, Aunt Katherine gave me a small section of a flower bed and let me plant anything I wanted. I chose radishes because of the bright red picture on the seed package. I didn't even like radishes, but I'll never forget the thrill when I dug up my first one.''

"That doesn't sound as if it would appeal to Don. I can't quite picture him grubbing around in the dirt.''

"You're right." Emily laughed. "He'd be the one lying on a chaise with a drink in his hand, watching me weed.''

"That's the best kind of togetherness. Each of you doing what you like best.''

Emily's animation died. "It would be nice. Too bad it's just wishful thinking.''

"You never know. The real estate market is depressed right now. It might make more sense to keep the house rather than sell in a buyer's market. Wait and see what the appraiser tells you.''

"What appraiser?''

"The one who came to see the house yesterday. Didn't your grandmother tell you? Evidently some of the family want to sell.''

"I didn't know." Emily stared at Sabena with a puzzled frown. "I can't understand why you don't seem to feel any resentment toward me. My family—and I—are trying to evict Martha, who is supposed to be your friend.''

"She *is* my friend, but neither of us holds you responsible. You haven't joined in the hard time the others have given her.''

"I've always had a good relationship with Martha," Emily said. "I don't want it to end in bitterness. I'm really sorry she's losing her home.''

"Don't be. Martha doesn't want to stay on. She'd planned to leave after she found someone reliable to take care of Lucky."

"I didn't know that."

"She didn't bother to tell any of the family, because they wouldn't have believed her, anyway. The only thing she wants is to find out what happened to Lucky. Martha feels she owes that much to Katherine."

"This whole mess could have been avoided so easily," Emily said with annoyance. "Why didn't Aunt Katherine just will Lucky to me? She must have known I'd take good care of him. He doesn't need money, he needs love."

"One sometimes buys the other," Sabena observed.

"Do you honestly believe that?"

"Maybe not, but I do know that money can make otherwise upstanding people do dishonorable things. Like kill a defenseless cat."

"None of my relatives would do a thing like that, and *I* certainly wouldn't." Emily's voice expressed indignation, but her eyes skittered away from Sabena's.

"I certainly hope not, but if Lucky is still alive, whoever took him should be persuaded to return him. They'll get their inheritance in time—without the risk of being blackmailed for the rest of their lives if someone equally dishonest should find out."

It was a long shot. Even if Emily knew more than she professed, Sabena didn't expect her to confess. It couldn't hurt, though, to put a scare into her.

Emily did indeed look startled. "You're talking as if real criminals were involved in Lucky's disappearance!"

"Whether it's shoplifting or grand theft, they're both criminal acts," Sabena said crisply. "You can't break the law just a little bit."

"I never thought of it that way," Emily murmured.

Sabena had planted the seed, now she wanted to move on. Emily would have to get back to work soon. "I'm afraid I'm a real hypocrite." She laughed merrily. "I've gotten a rash of traffic tickets lately, and I guess that could be considered breaking the law. Do you have to go to traffic school here when you get a speeding ticket?"

"I don't own a car. Don does, but we only use it on weekends."

"A BMW?"

"How did you know?" Emily asked in surprise.

"Just a lucky guess," Sabena answered blandly.

"I was so impressed when he took me out in it the first time. It's expensive to keep a car in the city."

"How did you two meet?"

"A friend of mine works in the investment department of a bank. Her supervisor was giving a party, and Judy asked me to go with her. She'd just broken up with her boyfriend and she didn't want to go alone. The funny thing is, she had to talk me into going."

"That's called kismet. Your eyes met Don's across the crowded room and you fell in love on the spot. Correct?"

Emily laughed. "Not exactly. I noticed him right away, but he ignored me completely. He told me later that it was only because he had to pay attention to the wives of important clients who were there."

"How did you happen to get together?"

"He called me a week later, just out of the blue."

"You must have made more of an impression than you thought."

"I doubt it. I think it was the big buildup Judy gave me when she met him again at a stockholders' meeting."

Sabena could fill in the gaps. After Don found out about Emily's connections, she became more desirable. Maybe that was unfair, though. Emily was a pretty girl and a nice person. She mustn't let her own tepid feelings toward Don cloud her judgment.

Emily was certainly enthusiastic about her fiancé. "I'd never met anyone like Don. He took me to all the best places, and we never had to wait for a table."

"He must have a good job."

"Oh, he does! Don is making quite a name for himself. He's very ambitious."

"That's admirable." Sabena tried—and failed—to sound approving.

Emily slanted a glance at her. "He's really a very warm person. Marguerite likes him a lot."

"Did Katherine approve of your choice?" Sabena asked casually.

Emily's smile was rueful. "Aunt Katherine didn't think anyone was good enough for her only grandniece. It had nothing to do with Don. She wouldn't have approved of anyone short of Prince Charles."

"He's too old for you."

"Besides being already married." Emily's smile faded as she said, "Don was very sweet to Aunt Katherine. He truly wanted her to like him."

"I don't doubt it."

Emily hesitated. "I'm sorry that you and Don got off on the wrong foot. You'd change your mind if you knew him better. Maybe the four of us could go out together one night."

"If you're including Jake, I'm afraid not. He's only an acquaintance."

"You had a date with him the other night."

"It wasn't actually a date. I asked him to take me to that gallery opening."

"He didn't seem to consider it a hardship."

Sabena shrugged. "He was simply being polite."

"Jake has wonderful manners, but I don't think he does anything he doesn't want to do."

Or even some things he *does* want, Sabena thought grimly. "I sort of got that impression." Her tone was ironic. "He's very controlled."

"That's the perfect word for him. Of course, he needs self-control to deal with my family. Aunt Harriet could drive anyone over the edge, but Jake hangs on to his temper—up to a point. Even *she* has sense enough to back down when he's had enough. There's something else about him," Emily mused. "In spite of all that charm, Jake is like an iceberg. An awful lot is hidden beneath the surface."

"I'm not interested in finding out," Sabena said tersely.

"You must be the only woman in town who isn't."

"Including you?"

Emily grinned. "Who knows, if I'd met him first. I'm only joking," she added hastily. "Don is an angel. I wouldn't trade him for anyone."

"They're both very... unusual."

"In different ways," Emily agreed, glancing at her watch. "Goodness, I had no idea it was so late! I have to get back." As they walked outside, she asked, "Are you coming back to the museum?"

"No, I spent all morning there," Sabena lied. "I think I'll go shopping and give the economy a boost."

As she walked down Fifth Avenue, Sabena reviewed her conversation with Emily. The signals she'd gotten were mixed. Emily seemed like a warm, decent human being. A little naive, perhaps, but basically nice. When she said she'd kill for the Fabian house, that was only an expression. Or was it?

Undoubtedly. Emily loved that cat. Her voice had a ring of sincerity when she said she'd never hurt him. What if someone was manipulating her, though? What if she'd been promised that Lucky wouldn't be harmed? There were two people who could convince her—Don and Jake.

Sabena scowled and walked faster. Of the two, she knew which would be her choice. The ice-cold one with the phony charm.

Jake was far from charming that morning. He snapped at everyone in a most uncharacteristic fashion. The secretaries walked softly around him, and a junior associate paused uncertainly at the door to his office.

"You wanted to see me, Chief?" he asked.

Carey Benson was young and nice-looking. Not spectacularly handsome like Jake, but someone with whom people felt comfortable. This was his first job since graduating from law school, and he was still a little in awe of Jake.

"What are you working on now?" Jake asked curtly.

"I'm finishing up the paperwork on the Chatterton litigation."

"Get somebody else to do it. I want you to help me."

"Great!" Carey's boyish face lit up.

Jake gave him a sour smile. "Don't celebrate until you hear all the evidence. Are you familiar with the Fabian case?"

"The one that involves the cat?"

"That's the one." Jake's firm mouth tightened even more.

"What do you want me to do?"

"Deliver some instructions to the Fabians. They're the kind of clients every attorney dreams of—in a nightmare. The entire case is a joke to begin with, and they're acting like the Three Stooges. There is a limit to my patience. That's why I want you to deal with them."

"You're turning the case over to me?" Carey asked incredulously.

"No, I'm appointing you liaison officer so I can concentrate on the legal aspects of the case. Which is what I was hired to do."

"I see." Carey didn't, but given Jake's present mood, he wasn't about to say so.

"I've just received information that one of them sent an appraiser out to look at the Fabian house. That was unwise, at the very least. Ownership of the house is still up for grabs. She...that is, the other side...thinks I sent him." Jake glanced out the window with a brooding expression.

"You want me to explain to the heirs that they're being a little hasty?" Carey asked cautiously when Jake didn't continue.

"I want you to tell them they'd damn well better stay out of it completely if they ever expect to see a thin dime. I've got clear-cut arguments for distribution of the estate, and I won't have them giving the opposition grounds for denial." Jake shoved his chair back and stood, shoving his hands into his pockets. "I want to wrap up this case and forget I ever met any of them."

"I'll get in touch with all three right away," Carey promised.

"All four. There's another heir, a grandniece named Emily. Add her to your list. You'll find their names and phone numbers in the file."

"I'm on my way, Chief."

When Carey was almost to the door, Jake said, "While you're at it, check out a little town in Wisconsin called Pear Blossom. Find out if—" After a long moment, he said, "Never mind. Forget it."

The door closed, and Jake wandered over to the window. He leaned against the wall, looking down at the snarled traffic without really seeing it. The face of a blue-eyed siren with glossy black hair blotted out everything else.

"Delilah probably looked like that," he muttered to himself.

Sabena's next stop was Don's apartment house. It was in a nice neighborhood, but not nearly as plush as the Fabians'. The building had no doorman. If the apartment was as small as Emily had indicated, Don was paying dearly for a good address and little else. Sabena rang the super's bell and waited a long time before he appeared.

The man didn't pretend to be anything but a glorified janitor. His work clothes were wrinkled and none too clean, and he hadn't shaved. His cranky expression lightened when he saw Sabena.

She smiled at him. "I was wondering if you might have an apartment for rent?"

"Sorry. Full up," he answered reluctantly.

"Are you expecting one? I have a friend living in this building. He told me someone might be moving out."

"Not that I know of. Who's your friend?"

"Don Scudder."

"Oh, him."

From his tone and the subtle change in his manner, Sabena gathered that Don had a lot of female friends. Or at least, used to have. But why not? She tried to be fair. Don had been a very eligible bachelor.

"Maybe Scudder was talking about his own apartment. He's getting married." The man watched her slyly to see how she'd take the news.

"So I heard. But he didn't say anything about moving. Maybe he and his fiancée are planning to live here."

"I wouldn't bet on it. These places are tiny. Most of the tenants are like Scudder. They don't hardly spend any time here except to sleep. And sometimes not even then." He winked at her.

Sabena hid her distaste. "He must come home to feed his cat."

"He don't have a cat."

"Perhaps you haven't seen it. He just got it. A little short-haired black cat."

"You got the wrong guy, lady. Scudder don't even like animals. He had a conniption fit when Meg Prescott's beagle jumped on him one morning. The pooch was only trying to be friendly, but Scudder said she got dog hair all over his slacks."

"Then I don't suppose he'd keep a cat in the house."

"Take my word for it."

"I guess I must have gotten him mixed up with someone else."

"Yeah. About the apartment—if you want to leave your name and telephone number, I'll give you a jingle in case anything opens up."

"Thanks, but I need something right now."

She left him and hailed a cab. Don was looking less than promising. That left only Charles.

Sabena wasn't happy with the way the case was progressing. True, she'd only begun, but timing was important. Jake was moving faster than she'd anticipated. The tried-and-true process of methodical investigation was a luxury she couldn't afford. After a moment's hesitation, Sabena leaned forward and gave the cab driver a different address, her home instead of her office.

She sat back, taking a deep breath. What she was about to do was questionable, but even a hotshot lawyer like Jake couldn't make any charges stick. Although, he'd undoubtedly try if he found out.

Sabena's stomach contracted at the thought of losing her license. Perhaps it would be wiser to consider all the risks first. But she didn't know how long Charles would remain in the Hamptons. It had to be today or never.

After the taxi dropped her at her apartment, Sabena went inside and changed out of the skirt, sweater and blazer that had been suitable for a day browsing the museums.

She emerged a short time later with an entirely different image. A silk scarf was draped artfully around the shoulders of her tailored suit, and her long hair was clipped to one side with a tortoiseshell barrette that matched her large round sunglasses. A collection of bracelets jangled on one wrist, and gold hoop earrings dangled from her earlobes.

Sabena shifted the bulky tapestry tote bag to her left hand and raised the right one to flag down a cab. The time for second thoughts was past.

The doorman at Charles Fabian's apartment building opened the taxi door and helped her out. He watched with discreet appreciation as she walked over and scanned the roster of tenants.

But when she pushed the button next to Charles's name, he asked, "Did you want to see Mr. Fabian?"

"Yes, I have an appointment with him."

"Mr. Fabian is out of town."

"That's impossible! We have an appointment at four o'clock."

The man looked at her sympathetically. "Maybe he meant *next* Friday."

"No, Mr. Fabian is in a big hurry for his new drapes. I'm an interior designer. I promised him a rush job if I could get in to measure the windows this week."

"I guess he forgot."

"Clients!" Sabena muttered. "They want everything done yesterday, and then they don't cooperate."

"That's the way it goes."

"The worst of it is, he'll blame me when the work isn't done on time."

"You can remind him that it's his fault."

"You know how far that would get me!"

The doorman nodded understandingly. "Yeah, these people don't like to hear things like that."

Sabena chewed on her lower lip. "I just started my own decorating business, and I was hoping Mr. Fabian might recommend me to his friends if he was satisfied with my work. I really hate to disappoint him, but there's no way I can deliver if I don't get those measurements today."

"Looks like you got a problem."

"There might be a solution." Sabena gazed at him appealingly. "Mr. Fabian doesn't really have to be here."

"If you're asking me to let you into his apartment, it's out of the question. I could lose my job."

"I don't want to go in alone. In fact, I wouldn't consider it. You can come with me and stay till I'm finished. It won't take long."

"I couldn't leave my post."

"How about the manager?"

"I guess you could ask. Her apartment is on the ground floor in the rear."

Sabena was forced to go through her act again, to a less receptive audience. The middle-aged woman inspected her suspiciously.

"Not without Mr. Fabian's authorization," she stated.

"I'm sure he wouldn't mind. He simply forgot about our appointment."

"Then it can't be all that important to him."

"It is to me. But I can understand. You have your job to do." Sabena sighed and let her shoulders slump. "I only hope I don't lose *my* job. You don't know what it's like dealing with rich people."

"Oh, don't I? I could match you story for story."

"Nothing ever pleases them, even if you follow their instructions exactly."

The woman nodded. "And they want instant service, whether it's the middle of the night or early on a Sunday morning."

Sabena smiled wryly. "Now you know why he'll probably cancel the job."

"Well, maybe I can do you a good turn. How long will this take?"

"I'll be in and out before you know it," Sabena promised.

Charles's apartment was spacious, and the furnishings had once been elegant. They were a little shabby now. He could have benefited from a decorator's services.

Sabena glanced quickly around the living and dining rooms. No cat came running out to greet them, nor did she hear any sounds of one in the apartment—although it would have been difficult to hear much of anything, since the manager, who had introduced herself as Mrs. Magnussen, kept up a running commentary.

"It's about time he fixed this place up." The woman stared disdainfully at a faded armchair. "Most of our other tenants have showplaces."

"You won't recognize it when I finish here." Sabena took a tape measure out of her tapestry bag and measured the width of the tall windows overlooking Central Park.

"I guess now that his sister died, he can afford to do all kinds of things. She was Katherine Fabian, that eccentric millionairess, in case you didn't know."

"I thought she left all her money to her cat," Sabena commented casually.

"That's what the newspaper said. But maybe the heirs got some of it. He's been pretty cheerful lately. When Herman, the doorman, remarked about it, Mr. Fabian said he just made a killing. Seemed real tickled about it."

Sabena turned around abruptly. "A killing?"

"Herman thought he meant in the stock market, but he might have been talking about some kind of inheritance."

"That's possible," Sabena agreed.

As she walked through the dining room toward a swinging door, Mrs. Magnussen asked, "Why are you going in there? That's the kitchen."

"I just want to throw something away," Sabena told her.

The kitchen didn't look as if it was used very often. The countertop held only basic small appliances, and there were no houseplants or pieces of paper with scribbled notations.

Sabena longed to open the cupboards in search of cat food, but that wasn't possible with Mrs. Magnussen at her elbow. The best she could do was take a tissue out of her pocket, wad it up and open the doors under the sink. The wastebasket was empty.

She led the way into the bedroom with the manager close behind. This room looked lived in. Some of the dresser drawers weren't completely closed, and the top of a highboy was cluttered. But no cat, or any sign of one.

It was totally improbable that Lucky was in the closet, but Sabena was determined to make sure. How, though, with the manager watching every move? She walked over to the windows, thinking furiously.

"Don't you have to measure from the top, too?" the woman asked.

"The length is standard for ceilings this height," Sabena lied blandly. "Don't you just love these tall ceilings? This is a beautiful apartment."

"You should see some of the larger ones."

Sabena put away her tape measure and turned around to stare across the room. Two doors were separated by a short section of wall. "Do they have better closets?" she asked.

"What's the matter with these. A single man doesn't need any more closet space."

"I was referring to the placement of them. Those doors cut up the wall. I'd like to make one big expanse with sliding panels, maybe mirrored ones. Unless there's a stud in the middle."

Sabena crossed the room and pounded hard on the wall, then listened intently. There wasn't a sound from within as there would have been if anything living was inside. Even Mrs. Magnussen was startled.

"Watch out! You'll go right through the wall."

"These buildings are solid." Sabena gathered up her purse and tote bag. "Okay, I'm finished. I can't tell you how much I appreciate your help," she said as they left the apartment.

Sabena walked away from the building, evaluating the latest evidence. Normally, Charles would no longer be a prime suspect. Except for his remark about making a killing. Was that just another example of a catch phrase? People used the expression for a number of things—like winning at the races. True, but Charles stayed on the list.

How would he react when he found out someone had been in his apartment? Mrs. Magnussen might not tell him if she had second thoughts of her own, but Sabena couldn't count on that.

Would Charles tell Jake? She felt a little chill of uneasiness. There was no logical reason for Charles to connect the incident to Lucky's disappearance. Unless he was the guilty one. Today's visit could force him into doing something foolish. At the very least, it would spook him enough to make him contact his lawyer. Would Jake suspect she was involved? He might if she made a point of avoiding him.

Sabena swallowed hard as she realized what she had to do. She found a telephone booth and dialed Jake's number.

He answered the phone himself. It was after five and the switchboard was closed. Jake's mood hadn't improved as the day progressed. He sounded tired and irritable.

"Hi, it's Sabena. Did I catch you at a bad time?" she asked, as though they were on the best of terms. "You sound busy."

"No, I . . . well, yes, I am rather busy."

"You work too hard. How would you like to buy me a drink? I'm right around the corner from you."

After a moment's hesitation, he said, "I'd like to, but I have to finish the brief I'm working on."

"I'll meet you in your reception area in half an hour." She laughed merrily. "I lied. I'm not really around the corner." She hung up before he could answer.

Jake swore softly, but he didn't look seriously displeased. For the first time that day, his face lightened.

Chapter Five

Jake was waiting for Sabena in the reception area. One quick glance took in her slender figure and lovely face. "You look different every time I see you," he commented.

"I'm trying to get your attention," she joked.

"You had that the first time we met." His gaze shifted to her large tapestry bag. "Have you been shopping?"

"I've done all sorts of things today. I was at the Metropolitan Museum this morning. I met Emily, and we had lunch together." That was in case Emily mentioned it to him.

Jake raised his eyebrows. "You two seem to have gotten very chummy. Don't you feel disloyal to Martha?"

"Not at all. Emily and Martha have a good relationship."

"Still, it seems rather strange that you'd care to spend much time with Emily."

"I'm lonely," Sabena confessed appealingly. "That's the reason I keep pestering you, too."

"I wouldn't call it that," he murmured.

"You're being polite again." She sighed. "I guess I should have called off my trip when I found out Sally wouldn't be here. Other than her and Martha, I don't know anybody else in New York. I didn't think it would matter. There's so much to do here. But even a matinee isn't much fun without somebody to talk to during intermission."

His expression was gentle as he gazed at her drooping mouth. "I'm sorry."

She gave him a tremulous smile. "You've been such a good sport about it that I'm going to let you off the hook. You don't have to buy me a drink."

"Do me a favor and keep me on the hook. I'd like a drink, too, and I don't want to drink alone. Let's try the Four Seasons."

Jake held her hand as they walked down Madison Avenue to Fifty-second and across Park. Sabena knew he only felt sorry for her, but at least their line of communication was reopened. She felt curiously lighthearted as they approached a modern glass-and-steel building with a simple gold plate announcing the name of the establishment.

The Four Seasons bar was crowded with business people unwinding over a drink before starting home. Jake found a table in a corner.

"I've heard about this place." Sabena glanced around the room.

"You're probably referring to the restaurant. It's famous for changing its floral displays with the four seasons."

"I've read that it's spectacular."

Their conversation was interrupted by the arrival of a waiter, who took their drinks order. Afterward, Jake addressed her last remark. "I wish I could ask you for dinner, but I have a previous engagement."

"I wasn't hinting," Sabena answered swiftly.

She really hadn't been. Staying in touch with Jake was a necessity, yet she intended to keep their meetings impersonal and in broad daylight. No more dates, even in the line of duty. She wasn't going to risk having things get out of hand again.

"I know you weren't hinting," he said. "It was my idea. Perhaps we can make it one night next week."

"Let's just play it by ear," she replied evasively. "Did I give you enough time to finish your brief?"

He shrugged. "It can wait."

"I can't believe what I'm hearing," she teased. "I'd written you off as a confirmed workaholic."

"Not when I can be with a beautiful woman."

"There's hope for you yet," she said lightly.

"I'm glad you didn't give up on me." He paused for an instant. "My behavior last night must have seemed strange."

Her lashes swept down. "Must we talk about it?"

"I feel I owe you an explanation." When he didn't continue, she looked up to find him staring at her intently. "The trouble is, I don't have one. You're amazingly lovely, but I know a lot of beautiful women."

"I'm sure you do," she murmured.

"What is it about you that's so enchanting?" He seemed to be talking to himself. "Your nose is too short, and you only come up to my shoulder."

Sabena laughed breathlessly. "I never claimed to be perfect."

His eyes took on a topaz glow. "I wouldn't change a thing."

She steeled herself against his velvety tone. "That's good. I might be able to do something about my nose, but I don't expect to grow any taller at my age."

"How old are you?"

"That's a terrible thing to ask a woman!"

"Not when she's as young and attractive as you. I wouldn't ask Marguerite that question." He grinned.

Sabena was abruptly reminded of her reason for being there—business, nothing else. "I'm not even going to comment on that," she said coolly. "We get into trouble every time the Fabians are mentioned."

"I'm sorry I was irritable this morning, Sabena."

"You really put me in my place." She pouted slightly.

"Maybe I was disappointed that you seem more interested in them than you are in me."

She knew that wasn't the explanation. Jake had been cranky when he'd answered the phone. "You and I don't have much future together." She traced a wet circle on the table with her forefinger. "I'll be going home soon, and by the time I come back again, you'll have forgotten all about me."

She waited for the usual polite reassurances. When he didn't answer, she glanced up. Jake was looking at her with that odd expression again.

Then his face hardened. "You're right. I'm not a very good prospect."

"What are you looking for in a woman?" she asked.

"I'm not looking."

"You know what I mean. What would your ideal woman be like?"

His gaze swept over her finely modeled features. "She'd have big blue eyes and hair as shining as a raven's wing."

"Why won't you tell me?"

"Why do you want to know?" he countered.

"I'm just curious to find out what kind of superwoman it would take to throw a net over you," she answered carelessly.

"At least you admit that a close relationship between a man and a woman is a trap," he said dryly.

"I didn't say that. Do you mistrust all women?"

After an imperceptible pause, he said, "I appreciate women greatly. The world would be a drab place without them."

"That's not what I asked."

"What difference can it possibly make to you?"

"I'm merely trying to understand you. Did you have an unhappy love affair?"

He shook his head, smiling. "Sorry to disappoint you."

"Then why are you so wary?"

"When I was a little boy, my mother read me the story of Samson and Delilah. It made quite an impression."

"I don't think she meant you to take it so literally. Besides, you have nothing to worry about. Just stay away from women barbers."

"A man always has to worry about a clever woman. She can make him believe in fairy tales."

Jake had said something like that last night when things had started to get heated between them. Was that why he'd stopped? Because he felt more than a casual attraction to her? A little thrill of excitement zipped through Sabena.

"At least *I'm* no threat to you." She gave him a limpid look.

"How did you reach that conclusion?"

"I won't be around long enough to change your thinking."

"You underestimate your impact, little one," he said wryly. "I'm going to remember you for a long time."

"That sounds like goodbye, but I'm not leaving for another week or so. If I promise to disappear from your life after that, can I call you every now and then?"

A number of unreadable expressions crossed his strong face. "My better judgment tells me to run like hell."

"Even if I promise not to leave a forwarding address?" she coaxed.

After an inner struggle, he made up his mind. "Okay, it's a deal." Taking her hand, he rotated his thumb over the soft skin of her wrist. "We'll have one perfect week together."

She withdrew her hand. "That wasn't exactly what I had in mind."

"What *do* you want from me, Sabena?" He watched her closely.

"I just thought we could have lunch together once in a while. Or maybe you'd take an hour off and go window-shopping with me. You really need the relaxation."

"Perhaps you're right. I was going to work all weekend, but you've given me a better idea. I have a country house in Sands Point. How would you like to drive down there tomorrow?"

Sabena was familiar with Sands Point. It was an exclusive community on the north shore of Long Island. She had a fairly good idea of what Jake had in mind. Which presented her with the sticky prospect of keeping him interested without fulfilling his desire. Her obligation to a client didn't go that far.

"Why don't we stay here, instead?" she suggested. "There's so much to do, and you won't have to fight the traffic."

"I enjoy driving. I do it so seldom. It will be nice to get away from crowds for a while."

"Not for me. I love the hustle and bustle of the city. That's why I come here."

"You haven't seen my part of the Island. It has green lawns, dogwood trees and a private beach. We'll take a picnic lunch and build sand castles. Or we can have lunch at the golf club, if you'd rather."

"Do you play golf? When do you find the time?"

"Not as often as I'd like, but I hack around whenever I get a chance."

She gazed at his splendid athletic physique, guessing that he was simply being modest. Jake wouldn't be mediocre at anything.

"How about it?" he prompted. "Do we have a date?"

"I don't think that's such a good idea," she answered carefully. "It's a long way for lunch. If you went alone, you could spend the weekend."

"Meaning, you don't intend to spend it with me?" He chuckled.

"I'm just a simple country girl. We don't have casual affairs."

"You're about as simple as an atom bomb," he said dryly. "But I respect your decision. We'll only stay for the afternoon. How would that be?"

She wouldn't learn anything significant about the case. If Charles did contact Jake, it wouldn't be until after the weekend. But Sabena knew that nothing was going to stop her from accepting his invitation.

"It sounds lovely—as long as we understand each other."

He laughed. "That's debatable, but we should have a nice time."

Carey's original enthusiasm over the assignment Jake had given him soured fast. The only one of the Fabians he'd been able to contact easily was Harriet. It hadn't been a pleasant conversation. She was indignant that Jake had delegated responsibility to an underling, and even more furious at the order to stop meddling in the case—even though Carey put it more tactfully than that.

"Now I know why the chief turned them over to me," he muttered when he finally got her off the line.

If the others were like this one, it was going to be a long afternoon. He had to get in touch with each of them today, or worry about it all weekend. Carey didn't relish the thought of telling Jake on Monday that he hadn't done the job.

After repeated telephone calls, he eventually reached Marguerite. She wasn't as explosive as her sister, and she insisted that she wouldn't make a move without Jake's permission. Then she kept him on the phone, asking questions about when she could expect her money.

Carey finally had to give up on Charles, which only left Emily. He called her repeatedly at work, but when she hadn't returned his phone calls by four-thirty, Carey decided to pay her a visit at the museum.

A guard directed him to a small cluttered office where a young woman was tacking posters to a corkboard wall.

Carey admired her willowy figure and silky, light brown hair. When she turned around, his interest quickened. Her face had the natural loveliness of a flower.

"Can I help you?" she asked.

"I'm looking for Emily Crandall. I left some messages for her. She didn't return my calls, so I decided to come over and speak to her in person."

"I'm sorry. I've been so busy all day that I never got around to looking at my messages."

"*You're* Emily Crandall?"

She smiled at his astonishment. "What were you expecting?"

"Someone older." And more eccentric, although he didn't say so.

"I will be after a few days like today." She sighed. "We're assembling a new exhibit, and nothing has gone right."

"That's too bad," he said absently, gazing at her wide-set brown eyes.

"Oh well, it comes with the territory. What did you want to see me about? I hope you're not selling insurance." She smiled ruefully. "I don't own anything worth insuring."

"Don't worry. I'm not a salesman, I'm an attorney. Jake Waring sent me."

Emily's smiling face sobered. "What now? Has there been a new development in the case?"

"Not exactly. Jake simply wanted me to speak to all the heirs."

"What about?" she asked warily.

"Some of the family have been trying to hurry things along, and that isn't a very good idea. It could complicate matters."

"Could you be a little more explicit? I don't know what you're talking about."

"Somebody sent an appraiser to set a value on the Fabian house. To arrange for selling it, I presume. But that really can't be done until the court decides who owns the property."

"I heard a man was snooping around, but I had nothing to do with it. I don't—" She broke off as the telephone rang. "Excuse me."

Carey watched as Emily's pleased expression changed to disappointment. Her conversation was punctuated by long pauses while the person on the other end delivered unwelcome news.

"Can't you get out of it, Don? I was looking forward to tonight.... That's what you said the last two times this happened. I don't see why you're always the one who gets stuck.... I suppose that's true." This last was said grudgingly. "All right, I guess it can't be helped. I'll see you tomorrow." She hung up slowly, then turned back to Carey. "I'm sorry. Where were we?"

"We were discussing the Fabian house."

"It's a beautiful old place," Emily said wistfully. "Have you seen it?"

"No, I haven't."

"I used to play in the backyard when I was a little girl. Aunt Katherine lived there for so many years. I hate to see the house go to strangers."

"Perhaps one of your family will buy it after the title is clear."

She shook her head. "I'm the only one who wants it, and I couldn't possibly afford it."

"I don't have all the facts in the case. Don't you get a full share of the estate?"

"Yes, but the others would expect to be paid for their shares. It's out of the question."

"Maybe not. They might be willing to defer payment. Inheritance taxes can really eat into bequests that are paid out in a lump sum."

Emily grinned. "Aunt Harriet will have a coronary."

He returned her smile wryly. "Yes, I talked to her earlier today. She was quite . . . outspoken."

"Jake is the only one who can handle her. Why did he send you?"

"I'm glad he did. I got to meet *you*."

"You're very polite."

"I was being honest. I'd like to help you get the house." Carey had only a vague idea of how that could be accomplished, but he seized the opportunity to get to know her better.

"Aren't you the one who's rushing things? Nobody gets it until we find out what happened to Lucky."

"You think he'll be found?"

She fiddled with some paper clips on her desk. "It's possible. He might have simply wandered away to look for Aunt Katherine."

"That's one explanation. But even if it's true, a cat's chances for survival on the city streets are slim."

Emily bit her lip. "I don't like to think about it."

"I understand," Carey said soothingly. "You have to be realistic, though. If Lucky is declared dead, the house becomes part of the estate."

"Somebody said the same thing to me." Her face lit with eagerness. "Do you think I could possibly swing it?"

"I have some ideas I'd like to explore with you, but it seems to be quitting time." Several people had waved and called good-night through the open door as they continued down the hall. "Why don't we go out to dinner and discuss the matter?" he asked casually.

"I'm sorry, but I can't."

"You have a previous engagement?" He knew she didn't.

"No, but I'm engaged. I don't date other men."

"I wasn't asking for a date. This would be purely a business meeting."

Emily hesitated. "If your fees are as high as Jake's, I can't afford you."

"I wasn't drumming up business," he protested. "You're already a client. I simply thought I could give you a little advice."

"That's awfully nice of you." She looked at him indecisively.

"I'm a very nice fellow," he answered appealingly. "I'm good to my mother, I swear only under great provocation and I prefer the ballet to a wrestling match."

"That's the clincher." She smiled. "Don hates the ballet. He'll invent any excuse to get out of going."

"I'll be happy to take his place. Where would you like to have dinner? I'll take you anywhere you want to go, but I hope it isn't someplace French."

"We really *are* kindred spirits! Snails are at the bottom of my list."

"With or without garlic butter," he agreed, helping her on with her jacket.

They walked out of the office laughing.

Sabena expected Jake's country place to be a small cottage. He'd described the lawns and trees accurately, but the graceful two-story Georgian house was a surprise. It was set at the end of a long driveway that wound through a wooded acre. The back of the house faced the beach, as he'd promised.

"This is magnificent, Jake!" she exclaimed. "I don't know which is lovelier, the house or the grounds."

"Come inside. I'll show you around."

The interior was spacious and furnished beautifully. The living room was rather formal, but the den looked lived in. A big leather chair and matching ottoman had a good reading lamp alongside. They were placed at an angle to the slate fireplace that showed signs of being used often.

"Everything is so spotless," Sabena marveled, glancing at the dust-free tables and sparkling windows. "How do you manage that?"

"A nice lady in the village comes in regularly to clean. I phoned and asked her to put some food in the refrigerator, in case you chose a picnic over lunch at the club."

"Definitely a picnic."

"Good. Let's go see what Dora left for us."

The kitchen was large and equipped with every modern appliance. The cheerful breakfast room adjoining was really an extension of the kitchen. It overlooked the beach and the water beyond.

"What a great place to have breakfast." Sabena gazed out at a sailboat skimming over the blue water.

"That can be arranged," Jake murmured, coming up behind her and sliding his arms around her waist.

She forced herself not to overreact. "You promised there'd be no hanky-panky."

He nuzzled the soft skin behind her ear. "This is just an honest display of affection."

"I never thought of you as an affectionate person."

He turned her in his arms. "I have hidden depths," he said in a silky voice.

"I believe you," she answered weakly. "Someone said you were like an iceberg."

"Don't you believe it," he replied softly.

Sabena knew they were poised on the brink. One tiny indication of willingness on her part would make this a weekend to remember. Jake would carry her to a bedroom upstairs, and they'd stay there all day. She would become acquainted with every hard muscle in his impressive body. And he would explore every hidden recess of hers. The vivid picture made her tremble.

Jake's sensuous expression vanished, and he released her immediately. "Shall we see what there is for lunch?" he asked.

Dora had laid in a lavish amount of cold meat, cheese and salads. She'd also provided bread and dessert, an assortment of French pastries.

"How many people did you tell her you were bringing?" Sabena exclaimed, eyeing the abundance of food.

"I didn't say."

"You should have told her there would just be the two of us, and only for lunch." The refrigerator was also stocked with bacon and eggs, steaks and much more.

"And destroy her illusions?" Jake grinned. "Dora thinks I hold orgies here."

"Do you?"

"That's not my style. One beautiful woman is enough for me," he answered meltingly.

"One at a time," Sabena observed dryly.

Jake didn't dispute the point. He was busy gathering bottles and jars from a cupboard. "Mustard on the ham, and mayo on the turkey?"

"That's fine. What can I do to help?"

"Not a thing. You're a guest."

Sabena watched as Jake deftly laid out slices of bread, covered them with meat and cheese and slathered the top slice with mustard or mayonnaise. Keeping up a steady rhythm, he sliced each sandwich diagonally.

"You do that like a professional," she commented.

"I used to be, more or less. One of my jobs in college was working in the cafeteria."

She gazed at his designer jeans, alligator belt and cashmere sweater. Jake was the epitome of a successful executive at leisure. "I can't imagine you doing kitchen duty."

He smiled mirthlessly. "That was one of my better jobs. One year, I worked in a fraternity house, washing dishes and doing laundry for overprivileged rich kids. I saw them get away with stunts that would have landed ordinary people in jail. But their daddies were always able to smooth things over. That's where I learned what success and influence can accomplish."

"It must have made you very angry," she murmured.

"Not at all. It was a good object lesson." He held up two jars of pickles. "Sweet or dill?"

A casual observer might have been deceived, but Sabena wasn't. Little by little, the pieces of the puzzle were starting to fall into place. His contempt for weakness and his steely self-reliance were more understandable. Jake had never had anyone to pick him up, so he made sure not to stumble.

"Okay, that takes care of the sandwiches," he announced. "Now I have to find where Dora put the picnic basket."

They spread a blanket on the sand and sat cross-legged, facing each other. It was a beautiful spring day with seabirds swooping overhead in the clear blue sky, their cries blending with the sound of the surf breaking along the shore.

Sabena took a bite out of her turkey sandwich and chewed reflectively. "I wonder why food always tastes better outdoors?"

"For the same reason that it's stimulating to make love in front of a roaring fire, or on the grass under a full moon." He smiled. "It isn't routine."

"I'll take your word for it," she said primly.

"Haven't you ever—" He stopped abruptly, looking amused. "I'm sorry. I didn't mean to embarrass you."

"You didn't." She was afraid her pink cheeks proved otherwise, but she brazened it out. "I simply prefer not to talk about my personal life."

"Poor Sabena." He chuckled. "What unimaginative lovers you must have had."

"Is this where you offer to further my education?" She tried to sound as amused as he.

"Perhaps in front of the fireplace. It's a little cool yet to make love outdoors."

"Besides, we'll be gone long before the moon comes up," she remarked lightly.

"Then I'll just have to think of some other way to amuse you. Do you have any suggestions?"

"You promised me a sand castle."

"And I'm a man of my word." He extended his hand to help her up.

Sabena's tension gradually subsided as she and Jake built a huge castle with rounded towers on all four corners. The tops were crenellated, and flags made from paper napkins fluttered from the ramparts. As a finishing touch, they dug a deep moat all the way around.

"Very impressive," Jake pronounced with satisfaction.

Sabena leaned back on her elbows, surveying their creation with equal approval. "I wonder what it was like to live in a castle."

"Cold and drafty. They didn't have central heating or electric blankets in those days."

"Those were minor inconveniences," she said dismissively. "Think of all the pluses—the fancy-dress balls with everyone wearing satin and lace."

"They probably had on long johns underneath."

"That's the difference between us. Where I see gracious living, you see long underwear."

"I'm a realist."

"I never could see what was so great about facing facts," she grumbled.

"It saves a lot of disappointments." He pulled her to her feet. "We'd better go in, you're shivering."

She wasn't aware of it until then, but there was a definite nip in the air. The sun was sinking to the horizon, taking its warmth with it.

"I can't believe how fast the time passed," Sabena exclaimed. "It seems we just had lunch a little while ago."

"Not to me. I'm getting hungry again. Why don't we have a drink and then I'll barbecue a couple of steaks?"

"They'd get cold before you got them inside. Ask me in the summer when it's warmer."

"You won't be here." He gazed at her with a slight frown. "Or will you?"

"You never can tell." She stooped over hastily. "Take the other two ends and I'll help you shake out the blanket."

Sabena continued to shiver, even after they went into the house. Her socks and the knees of her jeans had gotten damp from the wet sand.

Jake chafed her chilled hands between his. "You really are cold. I'll light a fire in the fireplace. That will thaw you out." At the look on her face, he started to laugh. "I meant that figuratively. It's the fastest way to warm up. Unless you want to get into a hot tub."

"No, a fire sounds nice," she murmured.

Sabena sat on a rug in front of the fireplace with her back against a sofa, watching as Jake touched a match to some kindling. When the flames began to lick around the dry wood with a crackling sound, he pulled off her shoes and socks.

"Your socks are wet. That's what's making you so cold." He massaged her feet vigorously. "Your toes are like little chunks of ice."

"My nose, too."

"I'll get around to that in a minute."

She smiled. "What are you going to do, rub my nose?"

"If necessary."

Jake continued to knead her feet until the blood started to circulate. "There, that should feel better."

"Yes, they're starting to tingle."

He moved up to sit facing her on the rug. Resting his weight on the arm that crossed her body diagonally, he lifted her chin in his palm. "Now let's see what we can do about your other problem." He leaned forward and gently rubbed noses with her.

"Isn't this the way Eskimos greet each other?" she asked faintly, very aware of Jake's face touching hers, his body just a whisper away.

"I've heard it's the way they kiss, but I've always had my doubts." His lips brushed slowly across hers. "This is so much more satisfying."

His mouth closed over hers and his arms circled her waist. Warning signals went off in Sabena's brain, but there was nothing very threatening about a kiss. She didn't want to overreact and provoke Jake's amusement again.

That was a mistake. She hadn't reckoned with her own vulnerability. His mouth was seductive, promising limitless bliss. Sabena's entire body warmed as liquid fire raced through her veins. She tried to resist him, yet she couldn't bear to have him stop.

After a brief period of inner denial, she clasped her arms around his neck. Jake tightened his embrace, unleashing the desire he'd kept under control. His kiss deepened in intensity as he probed her mouth with symbolic intent.

Sabena surrendered herself to the sensation, alternately running her hands over his broad shoulders and tangling her fingers in his thick hair. This was what she'd wanted to do for so long. If there was a reason not to, it was drowned out by the siren sound of his voice.

"My sweet passionate Sabena." He eased her onto the rug, cradling her head on his arm while he gazed down at her with blazing eyes. "What have you done to me? I've never wanted any woman this much."

Pure joy flooded through her. She reached up and pulled his head down. Jake gathered her close, capturing her mouth for a drugging kiss that turned her liquid inside. She quivered as his hand slipped under the hem of her sweater.

"You have such an exquisite body," he said huskily. "I want to know every inch of it."

Raising her slightly, he removed her sweater. Sabena shivered as he traced the slope of her breasts with his fingertips, skimming the edge of her lace bra.

"Are you still cold, sweetheart?" he asked with concern.

"No, I…" Her body was heated to a fever pitch. "No, I'm fine."

"You're more than that. You're magnificent."

His eyes glittered as he unclasped her bra and uncovered her breasts. Lowering his head, he curled his tongue around one sensitive nipple. Sabena drew in her breath sharply as his warm mouth sent a bolt of sensation through her midsection.

"Do you like that?" His thumb moved in a slow circle around the other nipple. "I want to know what pleases you." When her lashes drooped and she didn't answer, he kissed her eyelids. "Don't be shy with me, darling."

"I can't help it," she whispered.

"You do want me, don't you?" He watched her closely.

"So much," she answered in a breathy voice.

"That's what I needed to hear!" He twined one leg around both of hers and clasped her tightly.

She was achingly conscious of every lithe muscle in his long frame. Jake would bring her pleasure she'd never even dreamed of. Sabena moved restlessly against him as her need grew in intensity.

"Lovely Sabena, you're finally going to be mine."

Unzipping her jeans, he pushed them partway down her hips. She could hardly breathe when his mouth trailed a line of sensuous kisses from her throat to her navel, with pauses in between.

He rubbed his cheek against the exposed part of her stomach. "Your skin is so soft," he said deeply. "I want to touch you everywhere."

"Oh, yes. I want you to." All her inhibitions had vanished.

As she reached out blindly for him, the telephone shrilled loudly. The unexpected sound startled both of them.

"Who the devil—?" Jake growled.

"You'd better answer it," Sabena murmured, trying to sit up.

He clamped his hands on her shoulders. "Forget it! I don't care who it is. You're the only one who matters."

The piercing sound was impossible to ignore. After staring at her for an indecisive moment, he scrambled to his feet, swearing savagely under his breath as he grabbed the phone.

"I was just about to hang up," Dora informed him. "Did I get you off the beach?"

"No, I—what is it, Dora?" Jake didn't try to mask his impatience.

She didn't seem to notice. "Did I buy enough food? I put a couple of steaks and a few other things in the refrigerator in case you decided to stay for the weekend."

"Yes, fine, that was very thoughtful of you."

"Just put them in the freezer if you don't use them. I left your change on the kitchen table."

"You didn't have to call to tell me that," he said explosively.

"That isn't why I called. I forgot my key. I always put it in my pocket after I open the door, but my arms were full of groceries. I must have dropped the key on the counter and forgot all about it. Do you want me to come by for it now? I'll need it to get in on Monday."

"No! You don't have to make a special trip. I'll leave the door unlocked for you."

"I wouldn't want you to do that. You never know who might happen by. Just put the key under the green flowerpot on the patio table. I'll be there first thing Monday morning."

"I'll do it! Whatever you say. *Goodbye,* Dora!"

Sabena's body had protested the interruption violently. But once her senses were no longer overwhelmed by Jake's potent masculinity, sanity returned.

How could she have let things go this far? In another couple of minutes, she would have been another notch on Jake's belt. That's all she was to him. He was the most exciting man she'd ever known. Under different circumstances, she could fall in love with him, but he wasn't interested in love. No one could get close to Jake except physically, and that wasn't enough for her.

She zipped up her jeans, fastened her bra and pulled on her sweater. When Jake returned, she was trying to smooth her tumbled hair. His eagerness died as his gaze swept over her.

"What happened, Sabena?" he asked quietly. "Did you get tired of waiting for me?"

"No, I...uh...I just realized how late it's getting." She tugged at her sweater, unable to meet his eyes. "I guess we should start back."

"Is that what you really want?" He moved near enough to torture her nerves.

"I think it's best," she murmured.

He hooked a hand around her neck and drew her face so close that she could see each spiky black lash surrounding his vivid eyes. One small step would put her in his arms.

"You don't really mean that," he coaxed. "Something beautiful happened between us."

Her nails bit into her damp palms. "What happened was your average garden-variety seduction."

His hand fell away. "Are you telling me you were an unwilling victim?"

How could she lie? It wouldn't do any good, anyway. Not when her passion had been greater than his. "No, I wasn't unwilling," she answered in a low voice. "I shouldn't have said that. I'm very attracted to you. I'm sure you know that."

"Then why did you change your mind?" He tipped her face up, forcing her to look at him. "What did I do wrong?"

"It isn't...anybody's fault," she replied haltingly. "We simply want different things from a relationship. Or I guess I should say, there has to be a relationship. I can't just fall into bed with someone, no matter how much I want to."

His expression changed. "You were the one who said we had no future together."

She was caught in her own trap. "I'm not explaining myself very well." She chose her words carefully. "I need to feel that I mean something to you, that I'm not simply a warm body, someone to satisfy your needs."

"You can't believe that!"

"I have no reason to think otherwise," she said sadly.

"Listen to me, Sabena." His hands clasped her shoulders. "I meant it when I said you're very special. No other woman has ever held this powerful an attraction for me. But I can't make a commitment, even to you."

"You mean, you don't want to."

"It's pointless to argue semantics. That's just the way it is. I've never lied to you. I didn't today. Why did it suddenly begin to matter?"

"You're a very exciting man, Jake. When you were making love to me, nothing else seemed important. But when I had time to think, I realized what a mistake it would be."

He was silent for a long moment. Then he stroked her cheek gently. "I'm sorry. It would have been quite wonderful."

"I know." She sighed. "Will you take me home now?"

"No." When she gave him a startled look, Jake smiled. "We had a great time today, but if I take you home now, this is the only part you'll remember. That's not the memory I want you to take away. We're going to Louie's for a fantastic seafood dinner, and *then* I'll take you home."

"I'm not dressed," she said doubtfully.

"As far as I'm concerned, you're *over*dressed." He grinned. "But you'll look fine at Louie's. It isn't fancy."

Jake's teasing dispelled the tension. His easy transition could indicate that making love to her was no big deal, but Sabena knew better. She'd felt the intensity of his desire. A sharp pang sliced through her. If the telephone hadn't rung...

Chapter Six

Dinner was a great deal more enjoyable than Sabena expected. Jake was at his most entertaining, and the food was delicious. As he had promised, the rambling, unpretentious restaurant on the waterfront was patronized by casually dressed locals. They came for the fresh fish and buckets of steamed mussels that Louie's was famous for.

After a leisurely dinner, Sabena and Jake lingered over coffee, laughing and talking. She was completely relaxed by the time they started back to the city. Knowing Jake wouldn't misunderstand, she didn't hesitate to request a favor.

"Would you mind coming in for a minute?" she asked when he pulled up in front of her apartment building. "The light in my—in Sally's kitchen burned out, and I can't reach it even when I stand on a stool."

"That's what you get for not eating your spinach when you were little."

"Spinach gives you muscles, not height."

"Then you made the right decision. You're perfect just the way you are." He draped an arm casually around her shoulders as they went inside.

"Would you like some coffee?" she asked, handing him a new light bulb to replace the burned-out one.

"Don't go to any trouble."

"It's no trouble." While he removed the fixture, she plugged in the electric coffeemaker.

A few moments later, Jake climbed down from the stool and flipped a wall switch. "That didn't take long. Anything else that needs fixing while I'm here?"

"No, that's the only one I couldn't handle."

"I'm not surprised. These are very high ceilings."

"It's an old building. They don't make them like this anymore. There are some inconveniences, but I prefer it to those modern little boxes with no character."

"You talk as though this was your own apartment," he commented.

"Yes, well, I visit Sally fairly often." She turned away to get cups and saucers out of the cupboard.

"How often?"

"Every chance I get." She continued without giving him an opportunity to pin her down. "Which do you prefer, modern or traditional?"

"Traditional can be charming, but there's something to be said for modern kitchens and bathrooms."

"But those can be remodeled." The strange way Jake was staring at her made Sabena nervous. She felt the need to keep talking. "Like the Fabian house. I was only in the powder room, but it shows what can be done."

"Yes, Katherine obviously put a great deal of money into it."

"She spent a lot of happy years there. It seems a shame to see the house go to strangers."

"It won't if her cat is found," he answered evenly. "At least, it won't for a number of years."

"How long will the court wait for Lucky to reappear?"

Jake gazed at her with an enigmatic expression. "I wondered if we'd get through an entire day without mentioning the Fabian case."

Sabena gave a tiny laugh. "I think we've done rather well."

"Yes, you've been remarkably patient."

"I don't know what you mean."

"Your first attempt failed when you almost got caught in your own trap. You weren't prepared to go that far for information, were you?" He smiled cruelly. "I'm quite flattered that I had such an unexpected effect on you."

"You can't honestly believe I was trying to trick you!"

"You're quite good at this." He folded his arms and stared at her consideringly. "The wide eyes, the shocked, indignant manner. That's almost as good as the performance you gave in my arms."

Her cheeks bloomed at the memory. "You know I wasn't acting," she whispered.

"Not after I put my heart and soul into it," he answered mockingly.

"You don't have a heart!"

"Maybe not, but at least I don't use my body to get what I want."

"What do you call what *you* were doing?" she flared.

His mockery changed to anger. "I was stupid enough to think there was something rare and beautiful between us. Congratulations, Sabena. It takes a clever woman to fool me that completely."

"I told you the truth, but you're too paranoid to believe it. You're sure the entire female population is in a gigantic plot against you."

"At least I know one of them is." His face set in grim lines. "What's your stake in all this? Did Martha pay you to worm your way into my confidence?"

Sabena couldn't admit she was a private detective. Jake would never believe Martha had hired her to find Lucky. He'd be more convinced than ever that she'd let him make love to her in hopes of keeping tabs on his strategy. It was a no-win situation.

"You wouldn't believe anything I said, so what's the point? I'd like you to leave," she said quietly.

"That's an excellent idea. Thank you for a most informative day," he said sardonically. "You'll forgive me if I don't suggest we repeat the experience."

Sabena was trembling when Jake left—for good this time. There wouldn't be any more picnic lunches or casual banter. That was for the best, but she wished they could have parted friends. Jake's eyes had held contempt when they swept over her before he left, and there was nothing she could say in her own defense. Nothing he'd believe.

Sunday was like any other day to Sabena when she was working on a case. She showered and dressed, ignoring the dull headache that was the result of spending a restless night.

Her first stop was the animal shelter. It had occurred to her that the shelter would be an inspired place to get rid of Lucky without actually killing him.

Only a skeleton staff was on duty, but the young attendant was very helpful. "We have every kind of cat you could want. You may find yours here."

He led her into a large room filled with cages of stray animals. Sabena's heart twisted at the sight of the eager little creatures pressing their noses against the wire.

There were several black cats, but none resembled the one she'd seen at the Fabian house. Either they were the wrong sex, or they had long hair or a spot of white somewhere.

"Maybe he was adopted. Do you have records for the last two weeks or so? I'm really desperate to get him back," she said appealingly.

"Sure, I understand. I'll check." The young man flipped through the pages of a large register. "Nope. We gave away a black kitten, but no adult cat like you described."

Sabena thanked him and left.

All that day and the next, she checked boarding kennels, not only in the city, but in the surrounding areas, as well. It was dull, painstaking work involving dozens of phone calls.

Most of them were fruitless, but occasionally she got a promising lead. One took her to New Jersey, and another to Connecticut. Neither cat was Lucky.

When she returned from one of her wild-goose chases, the red light on her answering machine was glowing. The message was from Jake. Sabena's pulse quickened at the sound of his voice, even though it was as icy as it had been the last time he'd spoken to her.

"I want to talk to you, Sabena," he said curtly. "Call me as soon as you get in."

She had no intention of doing any such thing. Their last encounter had been too painful. What could he possibly have to say that he hadn't already accused her of? He certainly wasn't going to apologize, and neither was she.

Jake left several messages that day and the next, but Sabena ducked all his calls. She put him firmly out of her mind—as much as possible. He wasn't an easy man to forget.

Sabena was rummaging for her house key at the end of a long, frustrating day when Jake appeared like an apparition. "What are you doing here?" she gasped.

"You wouldn't return my calls, so I had no other choice. I've wasted an hour hanging around here waiting for you," he said impatiently. Taking her key, he hustled her through the door and followed her inside.

"You must have gathered that I don't want to talk to you," she said stiffly.

"That's too bad, because you have some explaining to do. Why did Martha hire a private eye?" When she gave him a startled look, he said, "Don't bother making up another of your ridiculous stories. I had you investigated—which is something I should have done in the first place. I can't believe I got conned by a pair of big blue eyes and a soft little voice," he said disgustedly.

"I couldn't very well announce that I was a private detective. My work has to be undercover, but I didn't con you." She met his gaze directly. "I knew when I went to the country with you last Saturday that I wouldn't find out anything."

"What are you trying to find out?" He ran long fingers through his dark hair. "Martha knows I'm attempting to have the terms of the will set aside. But even if I succeed, she'll have plenty of notice."

Now that Jake knew she was a detective, he might as well know the rest. "That has nothing to do with it. She thinks one of you took Lucky. She hired me to find him and discover which one of you did it."

"You're including *me* in your list of suspects?" he asked incredulously.

Sabena gazed back at him calmly. "The Fabians are a bunch of comic-strip characters—except for Emily, and I think she's too softhearted to pull a stunt like this—although I haven't ruled her out. But you have the nerve and the intelligence."

"I don't know whether to be flattered or outraged. You're accusing me of having committed a crime! I'm an ethical member of the bar, for Pete's sake."

"We had a discussion about that. You said anyone was capable of anything if the stakes were high enough."

"I also said you were misguided. Do you remember *that?*" Jake started to laugh. "I thought *you* were the one who supplied Martha with the substitute cat."

Sabena recalled every vivid detail of their first date. "Is that what you meant when you said you'd try not to hurt me?" she asked uncertainly.

His face softened as he gazed at her. "Harriet is a pit bull. She'd want to prosecute if she discovered you were involved. The others might not have felt too charitable, either. I couldn't let you get away with it, but I would have tried to restrain them."

"I guess you're sorry to find out I'm innocent. You could have thrown me to the wolves and gotten your revenge."

"Are you admitting I have a valid grievance?" He watched her with narrowed eyes.

"No," she answered quietly. "I went out with you because I wanted to. As long as we're finally being honest with each other, why did you ask me?"

"I didn't intend to," he admitted. "You were becoming a disruptive element in my life. I thought about you entirely too much. I'd decided not to see you anymore."

"Why did you change your mind?"

He smiled ironically. "You said you were going home soon. Any temptation would be temporary."

"I've been a disappointment all around," she said wryly.

"I wouldn't say that." His voice deepened. "I'm glad to find my suspicions were unjustified."

"Which ones?" she asked with a slight laugh. "You've suspected me of so many things."

"What else was I to think? Your interest in the Fabian case was excessive. A lot more than mere friendship with Martha warranted."

"Now that you know, are you going to tell the Fabians about me?"

He frowned. "I hadn't really considered that angle."

"I can't stop you, of course, but I wish you wouldn't."

"I'm not sure that would be ethical. They are my clients."

"If none of them took Lucky, they have nothing to worry about."

"I still represent them."

"You *do* think one of them is guilty, don't you? How can you condone such a rotten act?"

"You're jumping to conclusions," he protested. "I never said I thought any of them were involved."

"It wouldn't matter to you if they were, admit *that*. You couldn't care less about what happens to that poor cat."

DETACH AND MAIL CARD TODAY!

BUSINESS REPLY MAIL
FIRST CLASS MAIL   PERMIT NO. 717   BUFFALO, NY

POSTAGE WILL BE PAID BY ADDRESSEE

SILHOUETTE READER SERVICE
3010 WALDEN AVE
PO BOX 1867
BUFFALO NY 14240-9952

NO POSTAGE
NECESSARY
IF MAILED
IN THE
UNITED STATES

"Frankly, I could almost wring his neck myself," Jake said grimly. "Every time the subject comes up, we argue."

"Because you're hard and unfeeling," Sabena answered heatedly.

"And you're obsessed!"

"I'm only trying to do my job, the same as you."

"I suppose that's true," he conceded grudgingly. "But I still think you're misguided."

"We're never going to agree, so why talk about it? I'm just glad we got the misunderstanding between us cleared up. I have ethics, too. I don't get information by seduction," she said reprovingly.

"You'd be a menace to the male population if you did." He gave her a lopsided smile. "Are we friends again?"

"Were we ever?" She sighed.

"Maybe not, but I'd like to be."

Sabena wondered if that was possible, but she chose not to debate the point. "Sure, why not?"

"Will you go out with me again?"

"That might not be such a good idea," she answered cautiously. "Our dates have a way of ending in disaster."

"Believe me, I don't want a repeat of the last one any more than you do! Let me make it up to you. Tomorrow night? If you turn me down, I'll know you haven't forgiven me," he coaxed.

She hesitated. "Why don't we have lunch, instead?"

"If you'd rather."

"Can we leave the time flexible? I have a number of things to do in the morning and I don't know how long they'll take. I'll come to your office some time between twelve and one. Is that all right?"

"Perfect." Jake paused with his hand on the door-knob, as though he had something else on his mind. But all he said was, "See you tomorrow."

Sabena wasn't sure she'd made the right decision, but she didn't regret it. Jake brought excitement and color to her life. As long as they both knew there wouldn't be any romance involved, what was the harm? A man and a woman could be friends, couldn't they?

She was too busy justifying her decision to realize that Jake hadn't promised not to give her away to the Fabians. Nor did he say flat out that his clients were innocent.

Carey was surprised and delighted to find Jake in a good mood the next morning. He had approached his superior hesitantly. "Can I speak to you for a minute?"

"Any time. Come in and sit down," Jake said. "What's on your mind?"

"I delivered your message to the Fabians. I would have reported back sooner, but Charles was out of town. I had to wait till he returned."

"How did they react? Did they give you a bad time?"

"You might say that. They're a very... unusual family."

"Tell me!" Jake answered fervently. "Well, with any luck we'll wrap up the case shortly."

"You expect to get a judgment in their favor?"

"I don't see how we can miss—barring some unforeseen occurrence."

"Like the real cat turning up?"

"I can almost guarantee that won't happen," Jake said firmly.

"Will the house be sold?"

"That's up to the heirs to decide, but I imagine so."

"This isn't a good time to sell," Carey remarked.

"That's not my problem," Jake said impatiently. "They can fight it out among themselves. As they probably will," he added. "I've never known them to agree on anything."

"The niece, Emily, seems quite reasonable," Carey said casually.

"You'd never know she was part of that family," Jake agreed.

"We had a long talk, and I found out she'd really like to hang on to the house."

"Her relatives would expect to be paid what their shares are worth. It would take all of her inheritance, and maybe more. I doubt if her fiancé would approve."

"What's he like?"

"I suppose women consider him good-looking."

Carey had caught the distaste in Jake's voice. "Besides that. What kind of person is he?"

"A total jerk, in my opinion. All surface and no substance."

"Too bad Emily can't see it. She's a nice girl."

"That's what falling in love will do to you," Jake observed sardonically. "It clouds your judgment."

"She isn't married to him yet, so he shouldn't have any say about what she does with her own money. I think she's entitled to the house, if that's what she wants."

"Don't put yourself in the middle," Jake advised. "You'll wind up being the bad guy."

"I only gave her my professional opinion," Carey said defensively. "Emily was very grateful when I told her I might be able to work out a deferred payment plan."

Jake's eyes held a glint of amusement. "That's a novel approach."

Carey looked uncomfortable. "I don't know what you mean. I thought we were supposed to keep our clients happy."

"By all means. And while you're at it, see if you can keep the older Fabians in a reasonably good mood, as well." The telephone on Jake's desk rang, bringing their conference to an end.

Sabena's first stop that morning was the Fabian house. She felt honor-bound to have a frank talk with Martha.

The older woman greeted her eagerly. "You have good news?"

"I'm afraid not," Sabena admitted reluctantly.

Martha's face fell. "When you telephoned and said you needed to talk to me, I thought you were onto something."

"That's what we have to discuss."

"Come into the breakfast room, and we'll have coffee." Martha sighed.

Sabena followed her to the cheerful room at the back of the house. The black cat was dozing in a patch of sunshine streaming through the window, but as soon as they appeared, he streaked to the pet door and out into the garden.

"I see he hasn't gotten any friendlier," Sabena commented.

"I'm afraid he never will." Martha poured coffee from an electric pot plugged into an outlet on a kitchen counter. "It's kind of spooky," she said, carrying the cups to the table. "He looks so much like Lucky from a distance."

"Makes you kind of wonder what made Jake suspect that he wasn't," Sabena mused.

"This cat doesn't act like Lucky."

"But Jake didn't know him like you did."

"You still think Jake had something to do with Lucky's disappearance?"

"I'd like some concrete proof that he didn't," Sabena admitted.

"And I'd be surprised if he did. What about the others? Have any of them done anything suspicious?"

"Not that I've been able to discover. That's why I wanted to talk to you today. I know you don't want to believe it, but I honestly think Lucky is dead."

Martha shook her head. "The Fabians are greedy, but they're not stupid. Lucky is their insurance policy against any slipup in the plan."

"I haven't been able to find any," Sabena said grimly.

"I can't believe they were clever enough to commit the perfect crime."

Jake was, Sabena thought, but she didn't mention it again. "It looks like somebody did. I have to tell you, I think you're wasting your money."

"Let me worry about that."

"I feel as though I'm taking advantage of you," Sabena insisted.

"Are you only working halfheartedly?"

"Certainly not! I've been all over three states looking for that cat. I want to get to the bottom of this as much as you do."

"Then I'm getting my money's worth."

"I can't promise results," Sabena warned. "The fact that I've come up empty so far isn't encouraging. If I'm right and you're wrong, it's a lost cause."

"At least I'll know I did everything possible."

"Why is it so important to you? Katherine wouldn't hold you responsible. She knew what her family was like."

"That's beside the point. It's become a personal matter." Martha's jaw set squarely. "I can't bear to have people think I'm as mercenary as the Fabians."

"Nobody will ever know what happened."

"I hope not," Martha answered fervently. "You wouldn't believe what my life has been like since Katherine died. I can't even go to the grocery store without having someone stare at me and whisper. People I've dealt with for years treat me like some kind of freak."

"That won't last long," Sabena soothed. "Pretty soon they'll find somebody else to gossip about."

"Not if word got out that Lucky was missing, and I'm suspected of substituting another cat."

"Why borrow trouble?"

"Because I never know what's going to happen next. It's like living with a ticking bomb. Do you have anything even faintly hopeful to report?" Martha asked pleadingly.

Sabena couldn't lie, but she hated to discourage the older woman even further. She tried to put the best possible face on her negative results. "I can definitely state that Lucky isn't in Charles's apartment, and I'm ninety-nine percent sure that he isn't at Marguerite's or Harriet's, either."

"I'm glad you've eliminated Emily from your list."

"I didn't say that. I'm only telling you what I know for certain."

"I'm sure one of Katherine's sisters or her brother is responsible. Where else could they be keeping him?"

Sabena told her about the boarding kennels she'd investigated. "Unfortunately, there are a lot of them and they're scattered over a wide area. I still have a number of places to contact."

"If Lucky doesn't turn up at any of them, what else can you do?"

"My first priority has been locating him, not placing blame. If that proves to be impossible, I'll have to concentrate on finding out who took him. Once I know for sure, I'll put him or her under twenty-four-hour surveillance."

"You can't work around the clock," Martha protested.

"I can hire someone to spell me. Sooner or later, the guilty party will lead me to Lucky."

Martha looked at her doubtfully. "It seems to me that finding out who took Lucky is as difficult as finding where he's hidden. How do you intend to go about it?"

"I'm going to start by talking to some locksmiths."

"What good will that do?"

"Lucky had to have been taken out through the garden door. Do you remember what you were doing on the day he disappeared?"

"I had an appointment at the dentist's at one. I was gone for a couple of hours, but I was here the rest of the day."

"How about the Swensons?" Sabena asked.

"It was their day off. They left about ten in the morning and didn't return until late that night. They went to visit Greta's sister in New Jersey."

A bell went off in Sabena's mind, but she merely asked, "Was that their regular day off?"

"Yes, every Thursday."

"And do they usually stay away until evening?"

Martha nodded. "They like to get out of the city once a week."

"So, after you left for your dental appointment, someone could reasonably expect the house to be empty. The Swensons followed a regular routine, which the Fabians were apt to be aware of."

"They couldn't know I was going to the dentist that day," Martha objected.

"It didn't matter where you went. What someone had in mind would only take a few minutes. He or she simply had to watch the house and wait till you went out. If for some reason you stayed in all day, he'd merely have waited until the next Thursday. You were probably under surveillance from the moment the plan was concocted."

"It's hard to believe," Martha said slowly. "These are so-called civilized people."

"I'm sure that's what happened, though."

"If you're correct, why go to all the bother of taking an impression of the gate key? Why not just break in through a side window? The intruder would be shielded from the street by shrubbery."

"The house is protected by an alarm system. I noticed the metal stripping around the windows on my first visit. I'm sure you turn on the alarm when no one is at home."

"Yes, I do," Martha said.

"Besides, a cat can easily escape through a broken window. A judge might decide he'd merely been frightened off and could reappear at any moment. Lucky's disappearance had to be blamed on you, because you would only bring in a ringer if Lucky had died. That's what the Fabians are basing their challenge on."

"That's despicable! At least one of them knows I'm innocent," Martha said indignantly.

"We're going to try to find out which one."

"How can you possibly expect a locksmith to remember a single customer? That's their job. They make keys all day long."

"Not usually from an impression, though. A reputable locksmith would ask for a good explanation. He wouldn't want to be implicated in a burglary ring, which is what this would look like at first glance."

"I see your reasoning, but there must be hundreds of key shops in New York City. It would take weeks to visit all of them, and I don't know if we have that much time."

"I hope it won't come to that. For one thing, I'm going to concentrate on the ones most easily accessible to the suspects. Fortunately, the three older Fabians live in the same neighborhood."

Martha continued to look worried. "Wouldn't they go farther from home?"

"Not necessarily. We're dealing with someone who thinks he's supremely clever. I say 'he' because it's simpler," Sabena explained. "It could just as easily be a woman. No strength or special agility is involved. Anyway, this person is confident that you won't figure out how he was able to snatch Lucky, and no one else will even try, since you're the only suspect. Under those circumstances, why go across town to have the key made?"

"You'll still have to cover a lot of territory," Martha said dejectedly.

"Think positive. Maybe we'll hit pay dirt right away." Sabena tried to cheer her up, although she knew the legwork involved was daunting.

"That would certainly be a blessing." Martha smiled for the first time. "If Harriet is the guilty party, the locksmith won't have any trouble remembering her."

"Has she been bothering you?"

"None of them have lately. Jake must have spoken to them. For a while after Katherine died, one or another of them was here almost daily."

"What for?"

Martha shrugged. "You tell me. Probably cataloguing the furnishings to be sure I didn't make off with anything. The Fabians were all over the house."

"They must have given you some excuse."

"Flimsy ones," Martha answered tersely. "Like wanting to relive the happy times they'd had with dear, departed Katherine. I had trouble keeping a straight face."

"Did they go into the kitchen?" Sabena asked.

"I wouldn't know. I usually kept busy at my desk until they left. Greta or Lars could tell you more."

"I'd like to speak to them," Sabena said.

The older couple was apprehensive. As they all sat around the breakfast-room table, Sabena wondered if the Swensons' nervousness covered guilt, but she tried to put them at ease.

"This coffee is marvelous, Greta. What brand do you use?"

"It isn't the kind of coffee, it's the way you make it," the woman explained. "I put an eggshell in the bottom of the pot, and just a spoonful of egg beaten with ice water."

"This has egg in it?" Sabena looked at her cup incredulously. "It's so clear."

"That's the Swedish way. You try it." Greta was more relaxed.

"I will. Miss Fabian was fortunate. I'd certainly like to have you cook for *me* every day."

Greta gave her a melancholy smile. "Maybe Lars and I will be looking for a job soon."

"I'm sure you won't have any trouble finding one, but I thought Miss Fabian took care of you in her will."

"She was very generous." Lars answered for his wife.

"Then you won't have to work after you leave here. Whenever that is," Sabena added hastily.

"What would we do?" Greta asked.

"You wouldn't have to do anything. You could retire."

Lars shook his head. "Greta and I have worked all our lives. We enjoy it. We would get old and cranky if we had to sit around all day with nothing to do." He smiled affectionately at his wife.

"Is that the way you feel, too, Greta?" Sabena asked.

"Yes, Lars and I have talked it over. This place is home to us, but if we have to leave here, we'll find another family to take care of."

Sabena could finally cross them off her list without reservation. The Swensons weren't motivated by money. They had nothing to gain from Lucky's disappearance, and everything to lose.

"Perhaps you won't have to go, after all. I might be able to help if you'll answer a few questions for me."

"Anything at all," Greta replied fervently.

"In the week before Lucky disappeared, Martha says the entire Fabian family was in and out. Did any of them barge into your kitchen?"

"Every one of them."

"Wasn't that unusual? From what I've seen of the Fabians, they expect to be waited on. Why would they come in here?"

"Miss Katherine's sisters came through here one day on their way to the garden. They told me to bring them lunch out there." The housekeeper's mouth thinned. "I remember because I was in the middle of cleaning the oven and I had to stop. They wanted their lunch right that minute.''

''It figures. How about Charles? What was his excuse?''

''He came in for ice. He'd helped himself to a drink, and I guess it was too much trouble to fill the ice bucket from the freezer under the bar,'' Greta said primly.

''That's in character, too,'' Sabena remarked. ''What about Emily? Did she have occasion to pass through here?''

Greta's expression softened. ''She's a lovely girl. Miss Fabian was always so happy to see her.''

''Did she visit often?''

''She was very thoughtful for a young person. A lot of times she'd stop by on her lunch hour, or on her way home from work. And after she started to go with Mr. Scudder, they came for dinner quite often.''

''I got the impression that Miss Fabian didn't approve of Emily's fiancé.''

''I wouldn't know about that,'' Greta answered neutrally.

''Katherine was a little put out with Don for trying to sell her junk bonds,'' Martha explained. ''She knew more about the market than he did, but she put up with him for Emily's sake.''

''What reason did Emily give for coming over after Katherine died?'' Sabena asked.

''That was an act of kindness. She knew how lonely I was without Kathrine,'' Martha said. ''Emily would drop in just to chat and have a cup of coffee with me.''

''Miss Emily was a pleasure to have around. She used to watch me cook, and then ask for my recipes. I gave her dozens of them, but I don't know if she ever used any.'' Greta laughed.

"I'm sure she will after she gets married," Sabena remarked absently. Every member of the Fabian family had had an opportunity to make an impression of the key. It would only have taken a moment. "Did Mr. Scudder ever come over with Emily after Miss Fabian died?"

"Only once, and he didn't stay long," Greta said. "While Miss Emily was asking about Lars's bursitis, he paced around the kitchen like he was in a hurry."

So Don had had the same opportunity as the others. His pacing could be attributed just to his bad manners. Or it could be significant.

Sabena pushed her chair back. "I won't keep you any longer. You've both been very helpful."

As Martha walked her to the front door, she asked, "Did you find out anything useful?"

"Possibly. I'll let you know what develops."

Sabena went outside and hailed a cab, trying not to be discouraged. She had five suspects with opportunity and motive—six, counting Jake. "Please let it be Harriet," Sabena pleaded silently.

Chapter Seven

Sabena arrived at Jake's office about twelve-fifteen, but he wasn't ready to go to lunch. Although the receptionist said he was expecting her, Jake was involved in a serious discussion on the telephone. He glanced up and smiled briefly at her, then went back to his conversation.

Sabena hovered in the doorway, not wanting to interrupt. When he finally glanced over at her again, she whispered, "I'll wait in the reception room."

He put his hand over the mouthpiece. "Don't go. I'll be with you in a minute. There are some magazines on the table."

Sabena sat on the couch and picked up a newsweekly. She tried not to listen, but found it impossible. Jake was evidently negotiating with another attorney.

"We were willing to settle, but you preferred to play hardball. Now we'll let the court decide." For a moment, he listened impassively, then said, "The amount is nonnegotiable, Harry. If we have to sue, I intend to ask for double that amount."

The other man's reaction was so explosive that Jake held the receiver a short distance from his ear. Sabena could hear the caller's outrage from across the room.

Jake merely smiled. "I'm prepared to take that risk, Counselor. Are you? My client will make an impressive witness." Another pause. "I've given you all the time I'm going to. If I don't get an answer today, we intend to file suit." After listening patiently to the reply, he said, "*Today,* Harry."

Jake hung up and turned his attention to Sabena. "I'm sorry. It's been a hectic morning."

No trace of the ruthlessness he'd just displayed was evident on his face. But Sabena had seen the tiger with his claws unsheathed. It was a daunting sight.

"I have a couple of papers to sign, and then we'll have lunch. Where would you like to go?" he asked.

"Are you sure you're not too busy? We can make it another day."

"They're all like this." He laughed.

"You're a tough bargainer," she said tentatively.

"That's what I get paid for."

"But it's sort of a game to you, isn't it?" She gazed at his confident face. "You enjoy outwitting your opponent."

"Everybody likes to win."

"Do you have that strong a case?"

"You never know which way a jury will go, but I don't think it will come to that."

"You're willing to take a chance, instead of settling for a sure thing?"

He grinned. "You have to get some fun out of life."
The telephone rang. Jake answered it, then flashed a
triumphant look at her. "Yes, Harry. I think you made
a wise decision."

Sabena listened as Jake negotiated hundreds of
thousands of dollars for his client. She had to admire the
way he handled the victory. He didn't gloat or try to turn
the screws even more. Jake was a man of his word.

Would someone of his stature be involved in a dishonest act? Sabena wanted to cross Jake off her list of
suspects once and for all, but nagging doubts remained.
He could still be the mastermind behind Lucky's disappearance. The risk involved might appeal to this man
who lived life on the cutting edge.

Jake concluded his call with a rueful look at his watch.
"You must be getting hungry. I'm sorry I took so long."

"At thousands of dollars a minute, who could blame
you?"

He shrugged that off, reaching for some papers on the
desk. "I'll just sign these and we'll get out of here." The
intercom buzzed and he flipped the key, swearing under
his breath.

"I have the Jorgenson contract ready for you to look
over and sign," his secretary announced. "You promised to get it to him by messenger."

As Jake hesitated, Sabena got up from the couch. "I
picked a really bad day for you."

"I know it's boring for you to sit around here, but if
you'll just bear with me, I'll make it up to you."

"It's no big deal. We can have lunch another time,"
she told him.

"I have an idea," he said. "Why don't you go ahead
and get us a table at Giambelli's? I'll join you there
shortly."

"At the rate today is going, you won't be ready for lunch until dinnertime."

"Trust me. I won't be long."

His secretary appeared in the doorway, followed by Carey. "I'm glad I caught you, Chief," he said.

"You didn't," Jake answered briefly. "I have a couple of things to do, and then I'm having lunch with Sabena." He introduced them.

After acknowledging her politely, Carey turned back to Jake. "When you have a minute, I want to talk to you about the Fabian property. I think I've figured out a way for Emily—Miss Fabian—to take possession."

Jake darted a glance at Sabena. "I told you, you're being premature."

"It's only a matter of time until you break the will," Carey argued.

"That's by no means a sure thing."

"For you?" Carey laughed.

"We'll talk about it later," Jake told him austerely.

"Don't let me stop you," Sabena spoke up. "We don't have anything to hide anymore." She gave him a direct look. "Do we?"

"You know I can't discuss the case in front of you." Jake turned to Carey with a frown of annoyance. "Sabena is a friend of Martha Lambert, Katherine Fabian's former companion."

"I'm...sorry," Carey faltered, giving Sabena an apologetic look. "I was way out of line. Jake did tell me not to mix in."

"It's all right," she said. "I know Emily wants the house. We talked about it."

"But you're determined to see she doesn't get it," Jake said pointedly.

"That's a little harsh," Sabena protested. "There are a lot of reasons why I hope Lucky is found. But if he isn't, I'd be happy to see Emily take over. She's a very nice person."

"That's what *I* thought," Carey said eagerly. "She didn't ask for my help. I just felt the way you do."

"Emily would be delighted to know she has such a fan club," Jake remarked dryly.

"I was only trying to go the extra mile for our client," Carey said defensively. "That doesn't mean I don't have compassion for your friend," he explained to Sabena.

"Have you met Martha?" she asked.

"No, I'm not really on the case. Jake merely asked me to contact the Fabians on a little matter. That's how I met Emily."

"What did you think of the others?" Sabena grinned.

Jake was having trouble restraining his irritation. "Weren't you on your way to get a table?" he asked her.

"I have a great idea," she said. "Why doesn't Carey come along to keep me company? We can have a drink together." Her suggestion didn't please either man.

"I don't want to intrude on your date," Carey said.

"You wouldn't be. Jake is all tied up. He might not even make it."

"I'll be there," Jake said grimly.

"But when? Do come with me," she appealed to Carey. "I hate sitting alone in a restaurant."

"Well, the fact is . . . I sort of have a . . . an appointment."

"Oh, I'm sorry." Sabena laughed. "I'm intruding on *your* date."

"It isn't exactly a date. I mean, it isn't a date at all."
Carey cast an uneasy glance at Jake. "Actually, I'm
meeting Emily. Just to talk about a couple of things."

"Why, that's perfect!" Sabena exclaimed. "The four
of us can have lunch together."

Carey looked uncomfortable. "Well, I don't know
how Emily would feel about that."

"I know she wouldn't mind. We're very friendly. The
last time I saw her, she suggested we double-date. Of
course, she meant with her fiancé, but I'd prefer your
company. Wouldn't you, Jake?"

"I bow to your superior strategy," he answered sardonically.

"I'm sure that means yes." Sabena grinned. "Where
are you meeting Emily?" she asked Carey.

"At Pasquale's."

"Wonderful! I love their pasta. We'll see you there,
Jake."

Sabena wasn't sure if Jake wanted to keep her away
from Carey, or if he was annoyed at her for turning their
date into a foursome. She wasn't happy about that part
herself, but this was too good a chance to pass up. Carey
knew more about Jake than the others, and he wasn't as
cautious. She wanted a chance to question him before
Jake warned him about her.

As they walked to the restaurant, she remarked, "Jake
works awfully hard."

"You've got that right. He gives over one hundred
percent to his clients."

Sabena smiled at Carey's youthful hero worship.
"How can he give more than a hundred percent?"

"Jake does things that most attorneys wouldn't do."

"Like what?" she asked casually.

"Lots of things. One time he won an accident case, but the award was appealed. His client was a young man who wanted to use the money to get married and buy a house. Jake advanced him the down payment."

"There wasn't any risk involved," Sabena pointed out.

"There's always a risk. Judgments can be reversed. It isn't something most lawyers would do for a client."

"I'm sure you're right. It's kind of out of character, though. I got the impression that Jake doesn't think much of marriage."

"Not for himself." Carey laughed. "He says marriage is like getting a life sentence before you've even committed a crime."

"I'm not surprised he'd say something like that," Sabena remarked tartly.

"That's just the way men talk," Carey said hastily. "He'll change his mind when he meets the right woman."

"You don't have to spare my feelings. Jake and I are merely friends." At his look of skepticism, she added, "Really. If there was anything going on between us, would I have asked you and Emily to join us for lunch?"

Carey was instantly distracted. "You've met Emily's fiancé. Do they seem happy together?" He laughed self-consciously. "I guess that's a dumb question. I only asked because you and Jake seem to have reservations about him."

"I think Emily can do better," Sabena said bluntly.

Carey looked pleased. "Maybe she'll find that out."

"With a little help from her friends," Sabena answered demurely.

Emily was waiting for them at the restaurant. She showed surprise at seeing Sabena.

"I told Carey you wouldn't mind," Sabena said to her. "I hope that was all right. Jake will be joining us a little later."

"It's fine," Emily assured her. "I didn't know you two knew each other."

"We just met today," Sabena said as Carey went to inquire about a table. "He's awfully nice."

"Yes, he seems to be," Emily answered. "I don't know him personally. This is just a business lunch."

"I understand." Sabena's expression was guileless.

Carey returned to escort them to a table. The waiter presented large menus and then left them to make their selections.

"I can't decide," Emily said as she looked over the many choices. "I love the angel hair pasta here, but I also like their ravioli stuffed with veal and mushrooms."

"I'm having the same problem," Carey said. "Why don't we have an order of each and split them."

"You wouldn't mind?" she asked. "Don won't ever do that."

"Why not?"

"I guess he thinks it isn't very sophisticated." Emily laughed deprecatingly.

"I don't have an image to keep up." Carey smiled warmly at her. "I'll share with you any time."

Emily's cheeks tinged a delicate pink. She turned to Sabena in an obvious attempt to change the subject. "How much longer are you staying in town?"

"A week or so," Sabena answered vaguely. She was gratified to discover that Jake hadn't told the Fabians about her.

"I didn't realize you were only visiting here," Carey remarked.

"Yes, I love New York. Jake took me to see a wonderful musical the other night." Sabena wasn't anxious to talk about herself.

"Have you known him long?"

"Not very. I'm still finding out things about him."

"So am I, and I work for the man." Carey laughed.

"Is there *anybody* Jake lets into his confidence?" Sabena asked. Carey was proving to be a disappointing source of information.

"Jake isn't like other men," Carey answered. "He doesn't need anyone to help him solve problems, or give reassurance that he's on the right course. Jake is a law unto himself."

"You think he'd *break* the law if he thought it was for a just cause?"

"I didn't say that," Carey replied instantly.

"*I* think he would," Emily commented. "And I'll bet he'd get away with it."

"Ladies, be gentle," Carey pleaded. "The poor man isn't here to defend himself."

"Serves him right for standing Sabena up." Emily grinned.

"I still have hopes," Sabena said. "Let's all eat slowly."

They laughed and joked together over lunch as though they'd been friends for years instead of recent acquaintances. Emily and Carey were especially compatible. They kept finding areas of common interest.

Sabena watched with approval, hoping Emily would have the sense to realize how superior Carey was to Don. Her chance to help the cause along came when they were almost through eating. They were discussing the upcoming weekend.

"I have tickets for the ballet Friday night if you'd like to go with me," Emily said to Sabena.

"I'm flattered that you'd prefer my company to Don's." Sabena laughed.

Emily's answering smile was wry. "No offense, but he has to work."

"On a Friday night?"

"They're all the same to him." Emily sighed.

"Are you sure he's working?" Carey asked lightly. "You told me he'd do anything to get out of going to the ballet."

"You have a good memory," she said.

"I remember everything you tell me," he said softly. "Too bad you don't remember the things *I* say. I offered to take Don's place the next time he disappointed you."

"That's a good idea," Sabena said swiftly. "Let Carey take you."

"I couldn't do that," Emily protested.

"Why not?" he and Sabena chorused.

"Because I'm engaged. It wouldn't be right to go out with another man."

"Don't think of it as a date," Carey told her earnestly. "We both love the ballet, and you need someone to go with."

"I already asked Sabena," Emily answered uncomfortably.

"No problem," Sabena said. "Carey is the ballet buff."

"I invited you first," Emily replied firmly.

After a glance at Carey's crestfallen face, Sabena said, "Okay, I just had an idea that will solve everything. I'll ask Jake to take me, and the four of us can go together.

It can hardly be called a date if you're with your attorneys. Don certainly wouldn't object to that.''

"I suppose you're right," Emily replied indecisively.

"I'm sure of it. And maybe next time, he'll get his priorities straight." Sabena grinned.

"It's all settled then," Carey said with satisfaction.

"Not quite," Emily cautioned. "We don't know if Jake is free on Friday night. Or even if he likes the ballet. He might be like Don."

"Let's wait and ask him when he gets here," Sabena said.

She could have told her Jake wasn't anything like Don, but it *was* possible that he had plans for that night. In which case she'd think of some other reason to persuade Emily to go with Carey.

Jake didn't show up until they were having coffee. He was full of apologies to Sabena. "I'm really sorry. This was just one of those days."

"I have them, too," she assured him.

A waiter appeared with a menu, but Jake waved it away and ordered a sandwich and coffee. "You're very understanding," he told her after the man left.

"I know how you can make it up to her," Carey remarked artlessly.

"So do I." Jake smiled at Sabena.

"Don't you have something to ask him?" Carey prodded her.

"While he's feeling guilty, you mean?" She was amused by Carey's eagerness.

Jake looked at her questioningly. "What do you want to ask me?"

Sabena told him what they'd discussed. "It's rather short notice, but if you're not busy, it should be fun."

"Well, the thing is, I—" Jake paused as he gazed at Sabena's long-lashed blue eyes. "I can't think of anything I'd rather do than take you to the ballet," he finished.

"Then it's all arranged," Carey exclaimed with a happy smile. To ward off any further discussion, he asked Emily, "Would you like more coffee?"

"No, I have to get back to work," she answered.

"I'll go with you," he said. "I'm going that way."

After they left, Jake looked at Sabena with a raised eyebrow. "I always thought Cupid was a little boy."

"That's the general conception. What's your point?" Her expression was bland.

"Nobody would ever mistake you for a boy."

She smiled. "I'm glad you noticed."

"We established that fact long ago, and stop trying to change the subject. I get the impression that you masterminded our double date Friday night."

"Where would you get a notion like that?"

"Emily didn't seem completely happy with the idea."

Sabena grinned. "Carey was pleased enough for both of them."

"So you admit you're matchmaking. Doesn't it bother you that she's engaged to Don?"

"He isn't letting that interfere with *his* activities. Why should she have to go to the ballet alone when Carey is dying to take her?"

"For that very reason. You're not doing him any favor by encouraging his interest in Emily. Why get his hopes up for nothing?"

"You never know what might happen. Emily isn't married yet."

Jake stared at her with narrowed eyes. "You're a very devious woman."

"Not really." Sabena laughed. "I just like to do my bit to make people happy."

"Too bad that doesn't include me," he answered ironically.

In spite of Jake's reservations, the evening was a great success. They all enjoyed the ballet. Their seats weren't together, since they were purchased at different times, but they met after the performance and went out for a late supper.

"Wasn't the staging marvelous?" Emily asked. "I'm so glad you got to see this company," she told Sabena.

"I'll bet they don't have anything like it in Pear Blossom," Jake remarked sardonically.

"That's true. How did you like the performance, Carey?" Sabena asked hurriedly.

Jake obviously hadn't divulged her true identity to any of the Fabians, but he'd never promised not to. Maybe he simply hadn't had an opportunity yet. If so, she didn't want to give him one now.

"I thought the dancing was superb," Carey replied in answer to her question. "Swan Lake is my favorite ballet, and this was one of the best."

"It's my favorite, too," Emily said. "I just wish it could have a happy ending."

"If Siegfried really loved Odette, I don't think he could have been fooled by another woman," Sabena observed.

"It's a common occurrence," Jake said. "Men get fooled by women all the time."

"That's so cynical," Emily protested. "They were star-crossed lovers who couldn't help themselves. I think that's terribly romantic."

"Don't let Jake tease you," Carey said soothingly. "I'll bet he's as vulnerable as the next guy under that hard-boiled exterior."

"I wouldn't bet the farm on it," Sabena muttered under her breath.

Jake heard her, but his answer was ostensibly directed at Carey. "I don't see any virtue in being vulnerable, but I can be very romantic if the occasion warrants."

"You don't have to defend yourself." Emily smiled. "I'm just glad I was sitting next to Carey instead of you. We enjoyed every minute, didn't we?" she asked Carey.

"I've never enjoyed a ballet more," he declared.

They discussed dancers they'd seen in famous roles, comparing their interpretations. Both were very knowledgeable about the subject, and they rarely disagreed.

"It looks as if your little plan is working," Jake murmured to Sabena as the other two gradually left them out of the conversation.

"If it's this easy, don't you think she should have second thoughts about marrying Don?" Sabena asked.

"Don't ask *me*. I'm not a big fan of marriage."

"That's an understatement!"

He grinned. "You can't win 'em all."

"I gave you up as a lost cause the day we met," she said lightly.

His eyes scanned her lovely face. "If any woman could change my mind, you could," he said softly.

Sabena had to remind herself that he wasn't serious. "Even a country girl wouldn't buy that line."

His bemused expression vanished. "That's something we have to talk about."

"Later." She interrupted Emily and Carey's conversation. "Have either of you been to that new restaurant that just opened? It's called El Caracol."

"Doesn't that mean snail in Spanish?" Carey asked.

Emily exchanged a laughing glance with him. "Carey and I have a thing about snails."

"French cuisine isn't our favorite," he agreed.

"El Caracol isn't French. They specialize in Cátalan-style cooking, and I hear it's very good," Jake said. "I've been meaning to try the place. It's around the corner from my apartment."

"Let's all go there for dinner one night," Carey suggested.

"That sounds like—" Emily's animation suddenly faded. "I'll have to tell Don about the place. He likes Spanish food."

Sabena smoothed over the awkward moment. "You'd think New York had enough restaurants, but new ones keep opening all the time."

"They replace the ones that go out of business," Jake said. "Hope springs eternal."

They talked about their favorite restaurants and different kinds of ethnic food, but the former carefree mood was missing. After apparently forgetting her engaged status for an instant, Emily was constrained with Carey. The party broke up a short time later.

"Your scheme hit a snag," Jake teased Sabena on the way to her apartment. "Emily is feeling guilty about tonight."

"I'll bet she had a better time than she has with Don," Sabena answered.

Jake chuckled. "That's why she feels guilty. Nice girls aren't supposed to have fun."

"Emily won't have to worry about that if she marries Don."

"You're really down on the guy, aren't you?"

"He's one of those people who are easy to dislike, but you're right. I'm not being fair. From now on, I'm going to stop meddling."

"I'll bet!" Jake grinned. "You'd find it easier to give up Bloomingdale's."

"You don't have a very high opinion of me," she answered in an injured voice.

"On the contrary." His voice lowered to a velvety pitch. "I think you're utterly adorable."

Sabena regretted her complaint. They'd successfully avoided getting personal tonight—except for a few lapses—and she wanted to keep it that way.

"An adorable meddler?" she asked lightly. "Isn't that a contradiction?"

"Not in your case," he answered as they walked to her door. "I even like your vices."

He put his hands on her shoulders and turned her to face him. Sabena's apprehension was mixed with anticipation. This was what she'd hoped to avoid, so why did she want him to take her in his arms?

Jake's hands tightened as he gazed at her starry eyes and softly parted lips. After a tantalizing moment, he lowered his head and kissed her cheek. "Good night, Sabena. Thanks for an enjoyable evening."

She went inside, trying to swallow her disappointment. Jake always upset her in one way or another. She couldn't live with him, and she couldn't live without him.

The impact of that thought stopped her in her tracks. Was he more to her than just a charming, infuriating adversary? Had she fallen in love with Jake? No matter how fiercely she rejected the notion, the truth could no longer be denied. But what was she going to do about it? He'd made his intentions clear from the start. He didn't have any. She never knew when he'd get spooked and drop out of her life. Was that what happened tonight? Jake didn't say anything about seeing her again, not even that he'd call.

Sabena went into the bedroom with a feeling of hopelessness. Maybe that would be for the best. All she'd ever get out of their relationship was a broken heart.

Despite her apparent resignation, Sabena raced to the phone every time it rang the next day. It was never Jake. To make matters worse, she'd turned down a date for that Saturday night, so she had boundless time to agonize over her predicament.

Sabena vowed that Sunday wouldn't be a repeat of Saturday. She got out of the house early, met a friend for lunch and went to a movie.

The red light on her answering machine was glowing when she returned to her apartment after being gone all day. Sabena's eagerness faded after none of the messages were from Jake.

By Monday morning, she was miserable, but resigned. A clean break was more merciful than the constant turmoil she'd been going through. Jake kept reeling her in and casting her out like a yo-yo. That had to stop.

The phone rang as Sabena was going out the door. She picked it up without enthusiasm. Jake's deep voice made her grip the receiver tightly.

"I'm glad I caught you," he said. "I was afraid you might be gone."

"I was just leaving. What can I do for you?" Sabena was proud of her composure.

He chuckled richly. "You should know better than to ask me a question like that."

"I have a lot of work to do, Jake," she said evenly. "Could you come to the point?"

His voice sobered. "Is something wrong, Sabena?"

She didn't want him to guess! Her voice lost its edge. "No, I'm just in somewhat of a hurry."

"I'll only keep you a minute. I called to see if you want to try that restaurant we spoke about the other night. I hope you can make it on such short notice."

That reminded Sabena of the misery he'd put her through. Who had Jake spent *his* weekend with? She was angry enough to ask him. "What were you doing all weekend?"

"Thinking of you."

"You must think I fell off a turnip truck!"

"It's true, whether you believe it or not."

"I *don't* believe it. You would have called me."

"At the time, I thought it was better not to, but I'm tired of playing these high school games. I really want to see you, Sabena," he said urgently. "Will you have dinner with me?"

She could think of a dozen reasons to refuse, and only one reason to accept. "What time?" she asked.

"I'll pick you up at eight," he answered in a vibrant voice.

Sabena successfully rationalized her decision. She was bound to bump into Jake while she was on the Fabian case. If she severed all relations with him, their meetings would be awkward. When the case was over, their acquaintance would die a natural death.

She closed her mind to that eventuality. Nothing could spoil her mood that day. Not even her lack of success at one locksmith shop after another.

The ones closest to the Fabians were a washout. None of them had made a key from a wax impression, and they assured her they would have remembered. That left the entire city to cover, an almost impossible task without a small army of assistants. But she refused to spend any more of Martha's money, and until she got a more promising lead, this was her only hope.

Sabena didn't return home until almost seven. Her natural optimism was flagging somewhat, but the prospect of an evening with Jake made up for the unproductive day. She approached her answering machine reluctantly, not wanting to tackle any more problems.

Jake's message was the last one on the tape. "Call me at my office when you get in, Sabena."

Was he going to break their date? Disappointment knifed through her as she dialed his number.

He answered the phone himself, sounding impatient. That changed when he heard her voice. "I've been waiting for your call. Where have you been?"

"I just got in. Has there been a change in plans?" She tried to sound unconcerned.

"A slight one. I'm running behind schedule, as usual. Would it be okay if I picked you up half an hour later?"

Sabena's spirits rebounded. "No problem," she assured him.

"Great. I'd like to go home and get cleaned up first. I should be at your place no later than eight-thirty."

"Why don't I pick you up, instead? It seems foolish for you to come all the way over here so we can turn around and go back there. You said the restaurant was around the corner from you."

"It is. That *would* save time, if you don't mind."

"Not at all."

After she hung up, it occurred to Sabena that she could have suggested meeting Jake at the restaurant. That might be wiser. She hesitated, then decided against phoning him back. Everything was arranged. Changing the plan now would give undue importance to something that was perfectly innocent. Besides, she was curious to see Jake's apartment, and they'd only be there for a few minutes.

With a feeling of high anticipation, Sabena went into the bedroom to change clothes.

Chapter Eight

Jake's apartment was high up in a posh building on a tree-lined street. Sabena's footsteps were deadened by thick carpeting as she walked down the hall and rang the bell next to a paneled door.

After a longish wait, Jake opened the door. It was apparent that he'd just gotten out of the shower. He'd pulled on a pair of slacks, but his shirt wasn't buttoned and his hair was damp.

"Sorry to keep you standing there," he apologized, as he showed her into the living room. "I was just getting dressed. It will only take me a few minutes, though."

"Take all the time you need. I don't mind waiting."

She kept her eyes on his face, away from the broad, muscular expanse of chest revealed by his open shirt. A quick glance had shown her a dark triangle of crisply curling hair that tapered and disappeared inside the waistband of his slacks.

"I'll fix you a drink and give you some magazines to read. Make yourself at home. I'll be back in a jiffy."

"I'll wait and have a drink with you." She looked around the spacious room. "What a lovely apartment you have."

The living room had probably been furnished by an interior designer. The upholstered pieces echoed the colors in a brown, cream and white modern rug, and each table and lamp was the right proportion for the room. But there was none of the sterile atmosphere of a "showplace." Books crammed a built-in bookcase on one side of the fireplace, and Sabena could almost bet that Jake had selected the paintings. They were the eclectic mix of a collector.

"Would you like to see the rest of the place?" he asked, pleased by her approval.

"I'd love to if we have time. Will they hold our reservation?"

He shrugged. "If they don't, we'll go somewhere else."

The apartment was extensive. Next to the living room was a den, and beyond that a guest bedroom. They were both tastefully furnished, but the master suite was spectacular.

Jake's bedroom was tremendous, and the adjoining dressing room could have been pictured in a magazine. There was a place for everything. Shoe racks lined part of a wall that also held drawers and shelves. The hanging space was divided for long and short garments, and one circular rod rotated at the touch of a button.

"Now I know how pashas live," Sabena exclaimed.

"Hardly. They have slave girls to take care of them. I have to hang up my own clothes."

"Times are tough all over. Besides, slavery has been abolished, even in backward countries."

Jake grinned. "Okay, a pasha's needs are now filled by union workers. The point is, I don't have any of those."

"You have everything else." Sabena pushed the button to see the clothes go around again.

"Do you want to play in here while I go and shave?"

She glanced over at him. "You don't look as though you need to."

"Look again. Or better yet, feel." He took her hand and brought it to his cheek. "That's more than five o'clock shadow."

The fine stubble rasping against her fingers, coupled with his bare chest, emphasized Jake's masculinity even more than usual. Sabena's heart began to pound, and she snatched her hand away.

"You're right," she said brightly. "You could grate cheese on your chin."

"I'll be right back." He took off his shirt and hung it on a brass valet. "Pick me out a tie to go with a gray suit."

"How do you know I'm not color-blind?"

"I haven't found a flaw in you yet," he answered meltingly before disappearing into the bathroom.

Sabena remained in the dressing room, filled with poignant emotions. This was the way it would be if she and Jake were married. They would share their lives together. She wouldn't have to make jokes to cover her true feelings. She'd be free to run her hands over his splendid nude torso and kiss the hollow in his throat.

As she carried the dream a step further, Sabena's nails bit into her palms. It was never going to happen, so there was no point in torturing herself. Jake had been painfully honest with her. If she couldn't accept his terms, then she had to stop seeing him. How could that be any more painful than this?

Jake returned, clean-shaven and with his hair combed. "Where's my tie?" he asked. "You're still standing where I left you."

She forced a smile. "I didn't know you'd be so speedy."

"I told you it wouldn't take long." He rubbed his cheek against hers. "See? Smooth as a baby's bottom."

She inhaled deeply. "You smell good, too."

"So do you." He buried his nose in her hair.

Sabena's legs threatened to give way. She put her arms around Jake's waist to support herself. His response was immediate. Gripping her shoulders, he stared down at her dazed expression.

She made a desperate stab at self-control. Removing her arms, she said, "You'd better finish getting dressed. We must be terribly late for our reservation."

He continued to gaze at her with glowing eyes. "Do you really care?"

"Well, I . . ." She moistened her dry lips. "I suppose we should go."

"There's only one place I want to take you—to bed."

He jerked her close and kissed her with a raging hunger. Sabena was sucked into a vortex of swirling passion as Jake's mouth devoured hers. It was as though a dam had burst and all of his pent-up desire was let loose. While his tongue probed urgently, his hands skimmed over her body, intensifying her own longing.

Sabena fought a losing battle with common sense. This was what she wanted. Wasn't it better to follow her instincts than to regret it for the rest of her life? The answer was never in doubt. Twining her arms around his neck, she pressed closely against him.

Jake hugged her so tightly that she could hardly breathe. "Beautiful Sabena, why have we been fighting this?"

"I don't know," she whispered.

"It was bound to be. Sparks fly every time we're together. I can't get you out of my mind."

"Do you want to?" She dropped butterfly kisses over his face.

"I've tried," he muttered. "But you're like a fever I can't get over."

"Then don't try anymore."

She pulled his head down for a kiss that ignited both of them. Their bodies were taut with strain as they strove to get closer together. Finally Jake swung her into his arms and carried her into the bedroom.

"I've dreamed of this every sleeping and waking moment since you came into my life," he said hoarsely. "There's nothing I won't do to please you."

"Don't tell me, show me," she murmured.

"I intend to." He stood her on her feet beside the bed. "Over and over again."

Their eyes held as Jake slid the back zipper of her dress down. Excitement raced through Sabena like wildfire when he guided the garment over her shoulders and it slithered to the floor.

"This is what I couldn't get out of my mind." He traced the line of her collarbones tantalizingly, then dipped his head to slide his mouth over the curve of her breasts where they swelled above the wispy bra.

His sensuous touch drove Sabena's passion higher. She moaned softly when he removed her bra and stroked her breasts with his fingertips. Her entire body came alive, clamoring for him.

"You're more exquisite than I remember," he said huskily.

His lips circled one nipple while his hands slid down her sides to caress her hips. The feeling was even more sensuous somehow, veiled by her panty hose. She tangled her fingers tightly in his hair and uttered a tiny sound of delight.

"Your skin is like perfumed satin," he murmured, slipping his hands inside her waistband and stroking her bottom.

Sabena was reaching the limit of endurance. "Please, Jake, I want you so much." She reached for his belt buckle with shaking fingers.

"Ah, darling, that's what I hoped for."

Jake let her unfasten his slacks and push them down, along with his shorts, realizing the pleasure it gave her. But when her questing fingers found their goal, his restraint vanished. With a lightning movement, he stripped off her panty hose and clasped her so closely that their bodies were joined at every point.

When she moved suggestively against him, he groaned in sweet agony. Easing her onto the bed, he covered her body with his. She parted her legs in mute invitation, and for a throbbing moment they were poised on the brink.

Then he plunged deeply, filling Sabena with such joy that she arched her body into his. This was what she'd yearned to experience, and it exceeded all of her fantasies. Jake's driving power brought unbelievable rapture. The storm he created built in intensity until the crest was reached and a final burst of sensation washed over them, bringing blessed release.

They were quiet in each other's arms afterward, their heartbeats slowing gradually. Finally, Jake stroked the damp hair away from her face and kissed her gently.

"I hope you feel as wonderful as I do."

"Even better." She snuggled closer.

"I don't think that's possible."

They tried to put their feelings into words, then demonstrated them, instead, exchanging kisses and caresses. This tender sharing was as satisfying in its own way as their passion had been.

"How could I ever think I could give you up?" Jake asked softly.

Sabena smiled. "You certainly tried enough times."

"How about you?" He bit her ear playfully. "I wasn't the one who called a halt on that memorable day."

"That's all in the past."

"Why did you change your mind this time?" He scanned her face thoughtfully.

Sabena's lashes swept down. How could she say, because I found out I'm in love with you? Jake would be uncomfortable, at best. He didn't want her love. It would drive him away.

"I asked you a question, Sabena." His topaz eyes were suddenly watchful.

"What difference does it make?" She ran her nails lightly down his spine. "Are you complaining?"

"You know I'm not. I'd simply like to know what prompted your change of heart."

"You're just fishing for compliments," she teased. "You want to hear that your manly physique was irresistible? Okay, it was."

"I want the truth," he said quietly. "What changed your mind?"

"Do you cross-examine all your women like this?" she pouted.

"You aren't like any other woman I've ever known. Why is it so hard to get you to talk to me?"

Sabena knew she was no match for Jake. But he mustn't be allowed to get the truth out of her. She took the one course guaranteed to distract him.

Tracing sensuous circles on his buttocks, she murmured, "We can talk any time."

He tried to fight his awakening passion. "I have a feeling you're manipulating me again."

She touched him intimately. "Would you like me to stop?"

"You know the answer to that. A man is no match for a clever woman," he muttered as he wrapped one leg around both of hers.

Their lovemaking was less impetuous this time. Jake explored her body slowly, seeking out all the pleasure spots and lingering over them until Sabena flamed with desire. He fondled her breasts and kissed the soft skin on her inner thigh, delighting in her responsiveness.

"Do you know how happy it makes me to see you like this?" His eyes glittered as she arched her body urgently.

"I've never felt this wild," she gasped. "I—"

"Tell me what you want, darling," he said when she paused.

"I want *you,* Jake, all of you." That was as close as she could come to saying, I love you.

"My sweet passionate Sabena. You're mine now, and I'll never let you go."

Their union brought the same throbbing ecstasy and afterward, the same fulfillment. They drifted off to sleep, still curled in a close embrace.

Sabena awoke to find Jake staring at her with an unreadable expression. It changed to tenderness when her lashes flickered open.

"Do you know you make little noises when you sleep?" he teased.

"You're making that up," she protested.

"No, I'm not. You sounded like a kitten purring."

"That's because I'm so contented. Did you offer me a saucer of milk?"

"I didn't even give you any dinner." He kissed her, then threw back the covers. "Stay right there, I'll see what I can find."

"I'll help you."

"I'd rather picture you where you are." He pulled on a pair of briefs, giving her a sensuous smile. "It will give me an incentive to hurry back."

"Aren't you going to put on some clothes?" she asked as he started for the door.

"What for? I expect to take these off shortly."

"Where do you get your stamina?" she marveled.

"You inspire me." He grinned and left the room.

Sabena piled some pillows behind her back and glanced at the clock. It was almost one in the morning, but the nap had refreshed her. She felt vibrantly alive, and happier than she'd ever been. Jake might not love her, but for now, he was all hers. What more could she ask?

He returned a short time later carrying a large tray. It held plates of scrambled eggs and a stack of buttered toast.

Sabena sniffed appreciatively. "That smells wonderful. I didn't realize it before, but I'm starving."

"Nothing like a little exercise to work up an appetite." He grinned.

"Don't be lewd," she reproved. "Whatever happened to romance?"

"Can I have something to eat first?" he asked plaintively.

She laughed. "I insist on it. I want you to preserve what strength you have left."

"Don't worry about *me*." He leaned over and kissed her. "I wouldn't think of disappointing a beautiful woman."

Sabena pushed the scrambled eggs around her plate, unpleasantly reminded of all the women there must be in Jake's life. The one, or ones he'd spent the weekend with, for instance. She couldn't believe he'd spent those two days thinking of her, as he'd claimed. Sabena's cloud of euphoria dissipated. Was she just another in the sorority?

Jake glanced over at her. "You're not eating. I thought you were hungry."

"I am." She took a hasty mouthful. "The eggs are delicious."

He wasn't convinced. "I'm getting to know you pretty well, Sabena. Something is bothering you and I want to know what it is before this escalates into another mis understanding."

"Those are all behind us," she said softly.

"I hope so." He stroked her cheek. "I couldn't go through another Cold War. That's why you have to tell me what's on your mind."

"It isn't important." She forced a smile.

"Anything that threatens to come between us is important. Tell me what it is."

"I don't want you to think I'm possessive," she answered defensively.

"Why not? *I* am." He curved a hand around her neck and pulled her close for a satisfying kiss. "I'd feel very unfriendly toward any guy who tried to hit on you."

"Then you can understand how I feel about the woman you were with last weekend."

"What woman?"

"Come on, Jake! You didn't call me. I can't believe you were alone both Saturday and Sunday."

"You can believe it. I spent both of those days telling myself you were only interested in me because of the Fabian case, and if I had the sense God gave a goat, I'd better forget about you."

"But you called me this morning," she said uncertainly.

"Because I couldn't stay away," he answered simply.

"Oh, Jake." She smiled tremulously. "You're smarter than any goat."

When he reached for her, she went into his arms eagerly.

That was the beginning of the most idyllic period of Sabena's life. She and Jake spent every night together. It was almost like being married. They met at the end of the day and had dinner, either at a restaurant or at his apartment, where Jake did the cooking.

"You act as if I'm totally incompetent," Sabena complained. "How do you think I managed on my own all these years?"

"By popping a frozen dinner into the microwave," he said, taking the lid off a bubbling pot to peer at the fresh asparagus.

"Millions of people eat frozen dinners every night."

"That isn't dining, it's surviving."

"I feel so useless. There must be something I can do," she insisted.

"There is. You can kiss the cook." Jake's light kiss deepened when she put her arms around his neck.

The aching need for each other was always just below the surface. Often he would turn off the stove and carry her into the bedroom. Sometimes they had dinner at midnight, sometimes a hearty breakfast, instead.

The only area they disagreed on was the Fabian case. Sabena no longer believed Jake was involved, but she couldn't rule out the possibility that he had some suspicions of his own. Since the Fabians were clients, however, it was his duty to defend them—especially since he thought the will was absurd to begin with. They tried to avoid the subject.

The only other thing that came between them was their work. Both put in long hours, but not always the same ones. Sabena had to go when and where any new leads took her. It was frustrating when her schedule didn't jibe with Jake's. If it happened several nights in a row, they tried at least to have lunch together.

One day when Sabena stopped by Jake's office, his secretary said, "Mr. Waring is expecting you, but he's with a client at the moment."

"Oh, no!" Sabena groaned. "I have an appointment at two. Will he be tied up long?"

"I couldn't tell you. Miss Fabian showed up without an appointment, but Mr. Waring said he'd see her."

"Which Miss Fabian?" Sabena asked curiously.

The woman glanced down at a pad. "Her first name is Emily."

"I'll just stick my head in and say hello. Emily is a friend of mine."

After a perfunctory knock, Sabena entered Jake's office with a confident smile. Her reception wasn't what she expected. Jake's face didn't light up like it usually did. Of course he had to exercise restraint, but he seemed more distant than convention required.

Emily's behavior was equally puzzling. She was usually so friendly, but today she seemed uncomfortable. Her eyes slid away from Sabena's as she was saying hello.

"It's good to see you, Emily." Sabena decided she was imagining things. "How are things at the museum? Do you have any new shows I'd be interested in?"

"Only our permanent collection at the moment. I didn't know you were still in town."

"I'm having such a good time, I might never go home," Sabena answered lightly. She avoided looking at Jake.

"I'll be with you shortly," he said. "Perhaps you'd like to wait in the reception room."

"Well, sure," Sabena said uncertainly. She paused at the door. "Would you like to have lunch with us, Emily?"

"No, I...uh...I have to get back to work." Emily turned to Jake. "I guess we've covered everything. You'll let me know what happens?"

"I'll be in touch," he promised.

"What was the matter with Emily?" Sabena asked after she'd gone.

"I don't know what you mean," Jake answered. "She looked fine to me."

"I'm talking about the way she was acting—as if something was bothering her."

He frowned. "I thought you'd sworn off meddling."

"So there *is* something wrong! Are she and Don having trouble? Does it have anything to do with Carey?"

That would explain Emily's peculiar behavior, Sabena thought. She was the one who had encouraged the friendship with Carey.

"Forget about Emily and come here and give me a kiss," Jake said.

"You don't deserve one." She did as he said, anyway. "You were very cool to me when I came in."

"I was with a client."

Sabena gazed at him speculatively. "What did Emily want that was so hush-hush?"

"You know I can't tell you. Where would you like to have lunch? How about Chinese for a change?"

She ignored his attempt to distract her. "If you've found out something about Lucky's disappearance, you're duty-bound to tell Martha."

Jake's face set in the hard lines that always troubled Sabena. "I have an obligation to my clients and to the court. Martha is not my concern."

"Maybe not legally, but certainly morally. It would be cruel to keep her in limbo if you have information that would clear her name."

"That's what she hired *you* for," Jake said grimly. "Any discussion between us is a conflict of interest."

"I'm not asking you to reveal your strategy. We both know what you're trying to do."

"Then there's nothing to talk about."

"There is if you have knowledge of a criminal act," Sabena answered heatedly. "How can you protect a client who broke the law? And don't give me all that righteous nonsense about everybody being entitled to a lawyer."

"It happens to be true."

"Okay, so maybe it is, but I wouldn't want to live with that on *my* conscience," she muttered. "I suppose Emily came here with damaging evidence against one of your precious clients. That's why she couldn't look me in the eye."

"You're completely off base. That's all I'm at liberty to tell you," he said austerely.

Sabena knew that was only proper, even if she didn't want to admit it, but Jake's coldness hurt. Where was the warm and tender lover who was always so considerate?

"All right, we won't talk about it anymore," she said evenly.

"Thank God for small favors! Let's forget about the Fabians and have lunch."

Sabena couldn't switch off her hurt feelings that easily. They'd probably spend the entire time arguing. She glanced at her watch. "Actually, I don't have time for lunch."

"Will I see you tomorrow night?" He had a bar association meeting this evening.

"I suppose so."

"Don't put yourself out on my account," he remarked sarcastically.

Her temper flared to match his. "I won't."

His face was impassive as he watched her stalk out the door.

Sabena regretted her decision as soon as she reached the sidewalk. Damn the Fabians, anyway! Jake was right—they always provoked an argument. She debated returning to his office, then decided against it. They both needed a cooling-off period.

Sabena headed for the Metropolitan Museum, instead. She had to find out what was going on. Jake wouldn't tell her, but Emily was an easy target. Her only problem was finding a plausible reason for tracking Emily down so soon after seeing her in Jake's office. But this couldn't wait.

She needn't have worried about a believable excuse. Emily gave her a resigned look when Sabena appeared in her office.

"I suppose Jake told you." Emily sighed. "I hope you're not angry at me."

"Why should I be angry?" Sabena asked cautiously.

"Well, Martha is your friend. I feel badly about going to Jake, but Don was so insistent. And the situation does have to be resolved sooner or later."

This wasn't what Sabena expected. "What does Don have to do with it?"

"It was his idea. He has a chance to make a lot of money in the stock market. Not through insider trading or anything like that," Emily explained earnestly. "This is just a good investment in a growing company. But he needs capital to get into the deal."

"And he wants to use your inheritance," Sabena said slowly.

"It's for my benefit as much as his," Emily answered quickly. "I'd turn the money over to him to invest after we were married, in any case."

"Yes, I suppose you would."

"The problem is, this deal won't be around then. That's why I was in Jake's office. To see what he could do about getting me my share of the estate." Emily gave her a sidelong glance. "I guess I sound like the others."

Sabena shrugged. "You have a valid reason for needing the money."

"I only hope you're right about Martha wanting to leave. I'd hate to do anything to hurt her."

"Martha is solely interested in clearing up the mystery surrounding Lucky's disappearance, and proving she had nothing to do with it."

"I never really thought she did," Emily said.

Because she knew for sure? Sabena wondered after she left her. Emily now had an even more compelling motive. But suspicion wasn't enough. Sabena had to have proof, and she'd failed to get it despite weeks of exhaustive investigation. If this week didn't produce any results, she really should insist on withdrawing from the case. It wasn't fair to keep taking Martha's money.

Sabena was in low spirits that night. Her discouragement over the case was compounded by the foolish argument with Jake. She wandered around the small apartment like a lost soul. Television didn't hold her interest, and she couldn't concentrate on a book. Finally, she decided to go to bed so she could get an early start in the morning.

The doorbell woke her out of a deep sleep. A glance at the clock told her it was almost midnight. Pulling on a robe, she raced to the front door.

"It's Jake," he answered in response to her cautious question.

She opened the door. "What are you doing here at this hour?"

His glance took in her bathrobe and tousled hair. "I'm sorry if I woke you. You don't usually go to bed this early."

She smiled wryly. "I didn't have anything else to do."

His face relaxed in an answering smile. "I'm glad."

"That isn't very sensitive."

"I should have said, I'm glad you didn't look for someone else to fill your evening."

"It never occurred to me." Sabena was too glad to see Jake to play silly games.

He took her in his arms and buried his face in her hair. "I hate it when we argue."

"I do, too," she whispered.

After a most satisfactory kiss, he carried her to an armchair and sat down, cradling her in his arms. "I have a sure cure for what ails us. Let's promise never to mention the Fabians again."

Sabena smiled. "We'd find something else to fight about. All couples do."

"No, we wouldn't. We get along perfectly when we can forget they exist." He kissed her temple. "I was like a bear with the hives after you walked out on me today."

"It was your fault. You weren't very friendly," she complained.

His tender expression faded. "How did you expect me to act? Nobody likes to be used."

"That's a terrible thing to say!" She started to get up from his lap.

Jake restrained her. "Look at me, Sabena, and answer me honestly. Are you only interested in me because of the Fabian case?"

"You accused me of that before. How can you believe such a thing?"

"That's no answer." His face could have been carved from stone.

"You think I was pretending all those nights in your arms?" she asked incredulously. "Perhaps I'm in the wrong profession."

His face relaxed somewhat, but he still looked troubled. "You were willing to break our lunch date when I wouldn't tell you what you wanted to know. You even left tomorrow night up in the air.''

"I was miffed," she said penitently. "You were so distant. I wasn't sure you'd even care.''

His arms tightened almost painfully. "I care too damn much. I'm always afraid you'll walk out for good one day.''

Hope flared like a bright light inside Sabena. Had Jake fallen in love with her? He sounded like a man in love.

"I thought you didn't believe in long-term commitments," she said lightly.

"I don't know what I believe anymore," he muttered, parting her robe and cupping her breast. "You're enough to drive any man crazy.''

As she put her arms around his neck and parted her lips for Jake's possessive kiss, Sabena was filled with elation. All of her dreams were coming true—maybe even the ultimate one! Mrs. Jake Waring, she thought blissfully, before surrendering to his urgency.

Their lovemaking was both passionate and tender, given a new dimension by their quarrel. Both were anxious to please, to reassure, to give pleasure. Jake was inspired that night. He carried Sabena to the heights, using all of his expertise—his hands, his mouth, his hard body. Then he fanned the flickering flames and brought her new delight.

When they were curled up afterward on her single bed, Sabena began to chuckle. "You deserve a merit badge for making love on this narrow bed.''

"I had trouble giving it my best effort," he admitted.

She kissed the tip of his nose. "You could have fooled me.''

"Let's go back to my place," he suggested.

"It's so late, Jake. I don't feel like getting dressed."

"I don't want you to." He gave her a mock leer and caressed her body.

"Stop bragging," she teased.

"Okay, we'll get a good night's sleep, instead. You don't need to get dressed, just throw on a coat." He kissed her sweetly. "I like to have you next to me."

Sabena felt the same way, but she resisted the temptation. "I have a really busy day tomorrow and I'd like to get an early start. Can I have a rain check?"

"You have a standing invitation." He gave her a hug before getting out of bed.

In spite of her good intentions, Sabena overslept the next morning. Martha telephoned as she was getting dressed. The older woman was so upset, her voice was trembling.

"Has something happened?" Sabena asked in concern.

"Exactly what I was afraid of. Have you seen the morning paper?"

"No, I haven't had time to look at it. What's in it that I should know about?"

"An article accusing me of fraud, greed, deception, you name it. The story of Katherine's will is splashed all over the paper again."

"Try to calm down and tell me what the story says."

"Somehow the newspapers found out that Lucky is missing and another black cat was substituted in his place. When Katherine first died, all they reported was that she'd left her fortune to her cat. Now somebody ferreted out the actual terms of the will—that I was his caretaker."

"How could they find that out?"

"Maybe someone bribed a clerk in Jake's law office. It doesn't really matter. The article practically accuses me of a cover-up. My reputation is ruined!"

"This is just a passing phenomenon," Sabena assured her, because she didn't know what other comfort to offer. "It will all be forgotten next week."

"Not by the people I have to see every day. I always knew Jake was a slick attorney, but how could he stoop so low?"

"You think *Jake* gave the story to the press?" Sabena exclaimed.

"Who else? It bolsters his claim that the terms of the will no longer apply. The publicity is bound to pressure the judge for a decision."

"Jake wouldn't do a thing like that," Sabena insisted.

"It comes as a surprise to me, too. In spite of being on opposite sides, I really liked the man," Martha said sadly. "I didn't think he'd be this ruthless."

"I'm sure he isn't. Jake is a hard competitor, but he fights fair. There must be another explanation. Maybe one of the Fabians leaked the story."

"Their only reason would be out of spite. If that were the case, they would have done it as soon as the substitution was discovered. No. Jake is the only one who knew this would speed up the procedure. For some reason, one of them needs money fast."

Sabena was appalled as her defense of Jake crumbled. Even *she* couldn't shut her eyes to the facts. It couldn't be a coincidence that Emily was in his office just yesterday, lighting a fire under him. He certainly gave good service!

"I know you did your best," Martha continued. "But under the circumstances, I'm sure you understand why

I no longer require your services. Poor Lucky. It's all over with, and the Fabians have won."

"Not yet they haven't!" Sabena's eyes glittered with anger. "I'm going to stay on this case until I solve it, and it won't cost you a cent."

"It isn't a question of money," Martha protested.

"For me, either." Sabena's chin set grimly. "This has turned into a personal matter."

As soon as she hung up, Sabena phoned Jake's apartment. He had already left, but he hadn't arrived at his office yet.

"Have him call me the minute he comes in," Sabena ordered.

She paced the floor while she waited, filled with fury. No wonder Jake tried to make her promise not to mention the Fabians again. He wanted to avoid inconvenient questions. Jake had no conscience. It was unforgivable of him to calmly make love to her after destroying poor Martha. He would do or say whatever got him what he wanted.

Sabena snatched up the phone on the first ring.

"Good morning, angel." Jake sounded on top of the world. "Did you miss me as much as I missed you when I woke up?"

"I guess you didn't read the morning paper."

The tone of her voice made him pause. "No, I overslept and had to rush." He chuckled richly. "For some reason I was rather tired this morning."

"I don't doubt it. You had a busy day yesterday. Press conferences are so hectic." Her voice dripped sarcasm.

"What the devil are you talking about?"

"Don't try to stonewall *me!* Don't you think I read the newspaper? You knew how I'd react if you told me last night, so you simply neglected to mention it."

"You're not making any sense. What am I supposed to have done?"

"Do you deny telling a reporter that Martha tried to pass off another cat as Lucky?"

"Of course I deny it! Get me the morning paper, Helen," he called to his secretary. "Are you trying to say they got hold of the story?" he asked Sabena.

"As if you didn't know," she answered scornfully.

"This is the first I've heard of it, but you obviously don't believe me."

"How else would they know if you didn't tell them?"

"Reporters are regularly assigned to hang around the courts. One of them must have smelled a story and decided to dig deeper. He evidently discovered we're challenging the will on the basis of Lucky's disappearance." A rustle of paper told her that Jake was scanning the article. "I'm sorry Martha was named, but she isn't entirely blameless. She never came forward and said this cat isn't Lucky. We had to find that out for ourselves."

"A fine lawyer *you* are! You've convicted her without a trial."

Jake's voice had a biting edge. "I'm not the one with the closed mind. You've decided *I'm* guilty without giving me the benefit of a doubt."

"How can I have any? You're expecting me to believe in a lot of coincidences."

"I expected you to believe in *me*." He laughed harshly. "That was my biggest mistake. Well, you win a few, you lose a few."

Sabena felt an actual pain in her chest. How could she have thought Jake loved her? She'd never heard that note in his voice before, but she could picture his face—cold, hard and indifferent.

"You've never lost in your life, but I hope you do someday," she said bitterly. "It might make you a better person." She slammed down the receiver.

Jake remained motionless, staring at the phone for a long time. His face wore the same look of desolation as Sabena's.

Chapter Nine

Sabena was sincere in her promise to Martha. Jake and the Fabians mustn't be allowed to get away with their treachery. It would be easier to drop the case. Then she'd be sure of never having to see Jake again. But she couldn't live with the thought that her failure had caused Martha pain. If only she could wind things up quickly.

Sabena paced the floor, searching for some clue she'd overlooked. There didn't seem to be any. She'd considered every possibility, run down even the most tenuous lead. The only way she was going to solve this case was if the guilty party confessed, Sabena thought bitterly.

Suddenly she stopped pacing as an idea occurred to her. A way to flush the culprit out of hiding. Her eyes regained their sparkle as she raced to the telephone.

"Ace Investigations," a man's voice answered. "Peter Pulanski here."

"I've got a job for you, Pete," Sabena said without preamble.

"Ordinarily I'd be delighted, but wouldn't you know it? I'm up to my ears in work right now," he said.

"This won't take long. I just want you to make four phone calls for me."

He chuckled. "I can manage that, but you could get a secretary cheaper."

"Name your own price. All I ask is that you do it immediately."

"Sure, kid." He was impressed by her urgency. "Lay it out for me."

"I'll give you the names and numbers. This is what I want you to say to them: I know what you did. If you want me to keep my mouth shut, it will cost you fifty thousand dollars. Bring—"

"Whoa! Waita minute," he interrupted. "That's blackmail."

"Only if you intend to collect," she answered crisply. "One of these people is getting away with a crime. The innocent ones will probably hang up on you, but I'm hoping the guilty person will take the bait. Fifty thousand is chicken feed compared to what he stands to gain."

"What did he do? Knock over a bank?"

Sabena smiled. "No, he stole a cat."

"That must be some rare breed. Okay, where is the payoff supposed to take place?"

"Tell each one to meet you at the top of the southeast staircase overlooking the skating rink at Rockefeller Center, promptly at noon tomorrow. If they ask how to recognize you, say you'll find *them*."

"A public place is sensible, but you should still have backup. You're good, Sabena, but you're no match for a man, physically."

"This might be a woman."

He laughed. "No offense, but they can be even deadlier."

"Don't worry about me. I have this all planned out. Just get back to me as fast as possible."

"Will do," he said.

In spite of Pete's promise, it was late afternoon before he called back. "Sorry it took so long, but I had trouble tracking down a couple of them."

Sabena gripped the receiver tightly. "How did it go?"

"I got some interesting reactions. The one named Harriet had hysterics. She said I'd never get one penny from her."

"That doesn't necessarily mean anything. Harriet goes into shock when she has to shell out for a tube of toothpaste," Sabena said dryly.

"Maybe, but not once in her long tirade did she deny filching the feline."

"I'll keep that in mind. What about the others?"

"Charles Fabian huffed and puffed, called me a few names and then asked where I thought he could put his hands on that much money. He sounds like a winner."

Sabena's eyes narrowed. "Yes, Charles has been in the running all along. How about Marguerite?"

"The ditsy one? I don't know what to make of her. She seemed more interested in how a blackmailer works than the fact that I was blackmailing *her*. Of course it could have been a clever act."

"I don't know how bright she is in general, but she's plenty smart when it comes to her own interests."

"The young one, Emily, had the only normal reaction. She sounded scared."

"Like she had something to hide?"

"I wouldn't go that far. Ordinary law-abiding citizens don't normally have any contact with the criminal element. They're apt to freak out if they do. Then again, she might really be hiding something."

"Emily isn't at the top of my list, but I appreciate your input. Thanks, Pete."

"Anytime. Let me know how it comes out."

Sabena might have revised her opinion of Emily if she could have heard her conversation with Don. Emily phoned him as soon as she hung up after Pete's call.

After giving him the gist of it, she said, "I'm really frightened, Don. Lucky's disappearance is turning into a criminal matter."

"Don't panic. It was probably just a crank call."

"I don't think so. He sounded . . . menacing." Emily's voice quivered.

"He was bluffing. The guy probably read that article in the paper this morning and figured he could cut himself in somehow. It has to be a scam. He doesn't know anything. Did he give you any evidence to back up his claim?"

"No, it was a very short call. He simply asked for fifty thousand dollars to keep his mouth shut."

"You should have asked him what he knew that was worth that kind of money."

"I was too rattled. Do you think I should call the police?" she asked hesitantly. "Aren't you supposed to report threatening calls?"

"The police can't do anything about an anonymous phone call, and it will only bring more publicity," Don warned. "We don't need that."

"Lord, no!" Emily exclaimed. "It was embarrassing enough at work today after that article in the newspaper. Everybody thinks we're a family of loonies."

"I'm glad *my* name didn't appear. My boss is really stuffy. Any hint of notoriety could damage my career."

"I'm sorry if I'm a liability to you," she said stiffly.

"You know that's not what I meant, sugarbabe. I was thinking of both of us. I'm not the kind of guy who wants to sit back and live off his wife's money."

"I'm sorry, Don." Emily sighed. "That dreadful man really shook me up. I'll try not to think about him again."

"Well, it might be wise to find out what he knows."

"You're not suggesting I meet with him?"

"Don't worry, I'll go with you."

"I can't do it," Emily said flatly. "I'd be a basket case."

"You don't have to say a word. I'll do all the talking."

"What's the point, though? You said yourself, he can't know anything."

"We have to find out what his game is," Don said urgently. "Suppose he gets teed off at us for not showing up? He could start a rumor that we were involved somehow, and that could tie up the funds indefinitely. We're entitled to that money, and I'm not going to let anybody screw up the works at this late date."

"I just wish it was all over," she groaned.

"It will be soon," he answered soothingly. "Just don't lose your cool."

"Let's go someplace fun this evening and forget about everything," Emily said impulsively.

"I told you I was tied up with a client tonight."

"Can't you get out of it?" she pleaded. "I don't want to be alone."

"You don't have to be. Call one of your friends and go to a movie."

"I want to be with *you.*"

"I feel the same way, sugarbabe, but we'll be together every night after we're married."

"Are you sure you have time for a wife?" she asked sarcastically.

His voice deepened. "I know you're upset, darling, but everything's going to be fine. Trust me. I have to go now, I'm due at a meeting. I'll call you later."

The day seemed endless to Emily, even though all she faced after work was a long, dull evening. But at least she wouldn't have to pretend nothing was bothering her. When the phone rang near the end of the day, she answered it listlessly.

"It's Carey, Emily. Can you talk for a minute?"

She forced herself to sound cheerful. "Sure, Carey. What's up?"

"I thought you might be upset about that article in the newspaper this morning."

"You might say that," she answered ironically.

"Don't be. It's too bad some reporter got hold of the story, but it actually supports our claim. Jake expects the court to move for distribution of the estate."

"What if somebody had information about Lucky?" Emily asked haltingly.

"That would depend on whether the cat's alive or dead. Do you think Martha knows something she's not telling?"

"No, I wasn't accusing her, although that article makes her sound guilty."

"Jake is furious about the leak," Carey commented.

"I thought you said it helps our cause."

"He doesn't try cases in the newspaper. That's a shoddy way to practice law."

"This whole affair is shoddy!" Emily exclaimed. "Money turns people into monsters. I wish Aunt Katherine had left all of her money to charity. None of us deserves it."

"I wouldn't say that. You're just upset."

"So I've been told," she remarked bitterly.

"You need to go out and enjoy yourself. Are you seeing Don tonight?" Carey's voice was carefully casual.

"No, he's having dinner with a client."

"Your trusty stand-in is available. How would you like to have a hamburger and go to a movie."

"It's kind of you to offer, Carey, but you know I can't accept," she said regretfully.

"I don't know why not. We're friends, aren't we? What's wrong with a couple of friends taking in a movie together?"

Her conversation with Don ran through Emily's mind. That's what he'd told her to do, wasn't it? Emily knew she was rationalizing, but the thought of a long night of worrying about tomorrow's meeting was more than she could face.

"When you put it that way, I agree with you." A load seemed to lift from her shoulders. "I'd love to go to the movies with you."

The telephone lines were busy that evening. Harriet called her sister and brother, then Marguerite and Charles talked.

"What if the blackmailer has proof the wretched cat died violently?" Charles asked Marguerite in alarm. "We'll lose everything. The will says he has to die from natural causes."

"Are you telling me you were stupid enough to kill the little beast?" Marguerite demanded.

"Hold it right there! You're not going to point the finger at *me*. You could have done it just as easily as I."

"If I had, I wouldn't have left any evidence," she said angrily. "Everything was going just fine. The substitute cat threw suspicion on Martha, and nobody has been able to find the real one. None of us could have been held responsible. Now this comes up! You're a fool, Charles. You always were, and you always will be."

"Why would you assume *I* had anything to do with it?" her brother asked indignantly. "The blackmailer called all of us, remember."

"That's true. I wonder why?" Marguerite mused.

"Perhaps he wanted to get us fighting among ourselves. Exactly as we're doing now."

"I take it back. You aren't so dumb after all, Charles."

"Thank you, Marguerite," he answered with heavy irony. "You're my favorite sister."

"Is that supposed to be a compliment, considering my competition?"

"Much as I'm enjoying this repartee, I think we should get back to business. What are we going to do about the man's demands?" Charles asked.

"I thought I might keep the appointment," Marguerite replied casually. "I'd like to see what a blackmailer looks like."

"I suppose you want me to come along for protection," he said with equal lack of concern.

She gave a tinkling little laugh. "Your idea of a physical act is lifting a martini glass. What would you do to protect me, outdrink him? No thanks, Charles. I'm going alone."

Sabena was up at dawn the next day after a night of only fitful sleep. Her plan simply had to work! If it didn't, she was out of ideas.

Her nerves were wound tightly when she got out of a cab in front of Rockefeller Center at eleven-thirty. Glancing around, she walked swiftly down the long promenade centered by colorful flowering plants. Dozens of people were lounging on concrete benches or snapping photos. Others strolled along leisurely, gazing in the windows of the shops and offices that lined both sides of the mall.

At the end of the walkway was an airline office with a wide expanse of windows. Anyone standing inside had a clear view of the parapet overlooking the skating rink. Sabena went into the office and took up her post in a corner, shielding herself by the short projection of wall.

The minutes dragged by. Normally she would have speculated about the diverse mix of people parading by, trying to guess their professions and what they were doing there. But today all of her attention was focused on the observation point overlooking the rink. A deep voice in back of her made Sabena whirl around.

Jake was gazing at her without expression. "I thought you were behind this little charade."

The shock of seeing him rendered her speechless for a moment. Then she demanded, "What are you doing here?"

Sabena hadn't told Pete to phone Jake, because he was the one person capable of figuring out her plan. If Jake had taken Lucky, she knew he didn't make any mistakes.

"You're playing a potentially dangerous game, Sabena."

"So you came here to see I didn't win," she said scornfully.

"I'd expect you to say that," he replied without emotion.

"What other reason would you have?"

"I don't want you to get hurt," he answered quietly.

"So you *do* know what happened to Lucky!"

"I believe as I always have, that he died a natural death and Martha replaced him."

"If that's true, how could I be in danger?" Sabena asked.

"I'm not infallible. It's remotely possible there's another explanation."

"That one of your clients abducted him?"

"Or paid to have it done." He stared at her moodily. "In which case, he or she might also pay to have any threat eliminated. The money is almost within their reach."

Sabena barely listened to his reasoning. She was concerned with a more pressing problem. "You could only know about my phone call from one of the Fabians. I don't suppose you'll tell me which one called you?"

"*All* of them." Jake's smile was his first natural reaction. "Harriet wanted me to call in the FBI."

"Then they've all been warned off." Sabena was bitterly disappointed. She'd counted on the guilty party acting on his own. "Did you offer to come in their place? Or are you just here to gloat over my failure?" She was sorry as soon as the words were out of her mouth, but it was too late.

A look of pain crossed his face. It was replaced by one of austerity. "I think your conspiracy theory is off base, but if it should turn out to be valid, they won't sit idly by and let you snatch the prize from under their noses."

"If I can't handle a clutch of characters like the Fabians, I'd better get into another business."

"Has it occurred to you that they might bring in outside muscle?"

She looked at him uncertainly. "They aren't career criminals. None of the Fabians would know how to contact a strong-arm man."

"It's easy in a city like New York. There are dozens of sleazy bars where you can find somebody to do your dirty work, no questions asked. All you need is money— and they have plenty of it."

Sabena knew Jake was right. Had she erred in writing off the Fabians as a bunch of inept clowns? Even worse, had she misjudged Jake?

"I'm . . . sorry for the things I said to you," she faltered.

"Don't be. I'm not." His hard face didn't soften. "It's the first time you've been honest about your feelings for me."

"How can you believe that?"

"I didn't want to. I kept telling myself you cared, because I wanted so badly to believe it."

"Why did it matter, Jake? You had what you wanted out of our relationship." She gazed at him, searching for some sign that more than his ego was bruised.

"Perhaps I wanted more than sex. Men don't like to be used any more than women do."

"What more could I have given you? Love? That's the last thing in the world you wanted."

Something flickered deep in his eyes. "Are you saying that's what *you* wanted?"

Sabena's nails bit into her palms in an effort to conceal her true emotions. "I never expected love to be involved, but our nights together meant more to me than mere physical gratification. You don't believe that because you've never trusted me," she said sadly.

The light in his eyes had died with her first words. "You're conveniently forgetting your own suspicions about *me!*"

Honesty forced her to admit that was true. "I guess we were doomed from the start." She sighed.

"At least give up on the Fabians," he said urgently. "Let them have the damn money!"

"I can't," she whispered. "They've cost me too much."

Jake was too upset to grasp the import of her words. "It isn't worth risking your neck over. Go home, Sabena. You've done your best."

"You wouldn't quit if the deck was stacked against *you.*"

"I'm a fine role model," he said disgustedly. "I can't even make a success out of my personal life."

"You didn't mess it up alone," she answered in a muted voice.

He stared at her somberly. "It doesn't matter who's to blame. The important thing is your safety. I can't let anything happen to you."

She wanted to believe his concern meant he cared for her. But common sense told her Jake would feel responsible in some measure. Even if he didn't love her, he wasn't *that* callous. She glanced away to hide the tears that prickled her eyelids, then stiffened suddenly. Marguerite was walking by the airline office.

Noticing Sabena's taut pose, Jake turned to see what she was staring at. "Well, I'll be damned," he exclaimed.

Sabena forgot her personal problems in the excitement of the moment. "I knew my plan would work! Do you believe me now?"

"I don't know what to believe," he answered slowly.

"You told her not to come, didn't you? So this proves she's involved."

"It begins to look that way," he admitted. "I told her it was probably a trick, and keeping the appointment would only indicate she had something to hide. I told all of them the same thing."

"But she was the one who disregarded your advice."

They watched as Marguerite strolled unhurriedly toward the meeting place, dressed as though going to a fancy luncheon. Her suit was a high-style Oscar de la Renta with a frilly blouse, and her hair was impeccably coiffed.

Sabena continued to stare in fascination, but suddenly Jake pointed and laughed. Skulking along behind her was Charles. His attempt at concealment was ludicrous. Darting from one group of people to another, he slunk along in back of them, sneaking an occasional peek over their shoulders.

"What on earth is he doing?" Sabena asked.

"Begging to get arrested." Jake chuckled. "If a policeman came along, he'd either cart him off to the slammer or the nearest psychiatric ward."

"Does this mean he and Marguerite are partners in crime?" Sabena asked uncertainly.

"Not necessarily. Charles looks like he's shadowing her."

"Maybe to *you.*" Sabena couldn't help laughing along with Jake. "I'd say he was auditioning for a part in a slapstick comedy."

"I think another character has been added." Jake indicated the heavyset woman marching down the sidewalk.

Harriet's perpetual expression of annoyance was even more pronounced as she gained on Charles and tapped him on the shoulder. His yelp of surprise was comical. The ensuing shouting match between the two drew Marguerite's attention. She joined them, and all three exchanged heated words.

Sabena frowned. "Is it possible they're all in it together?"

"I hardly think so. Can you really see them agreeing on a plan, and then keeping their mouths shut?"

"It doesn't seem likely," she agreed. "But what are they doing here?"

"That's what I'm about to find out. Do you want to come with me?"

Sabena hesitated. "Wouldn't my being here look suspicious?"

"They're so busy fighting among themselves that I doubt if they'd even notice, but it's up to you."

"They're not going to admit to anything in front of me." She slanted a glance at him. "Will you tell me what reasons they give for being here?"

"Will you believe what I say?" he asked impassively.

"I deserve that." She looked away, unable to meet his gaze. "Besides, your clients come first. I understand that."

"You've never understood anything about me," he grated.

As she was searching for a reply, something distracted Sabena. "Well, the gang's all here," she said ironically, gesturing toward the group outside. Emily and Don had joined the others.

"I don't now what the hell they think they're up to." Jake shook his head helplessly. "I thought Emily, at least, would have better sense. Stay here. I'll be right back."

The Fabian family greeted Jake volubly, each vying for his attention. He restrained his impatience, trying to listen to each of them. When they persisted in all talking at once, he held up his hand and asked questions.

Sabena couldn't draw any conclusions by watching. Were they confessing to Jake? Excusing themselves? Would Jake tell her if they were involved? He couldn't, ethically. Every instinct urged Sabena to find out for herself what was going on, but she knew that would be counterproductive. They'd only close ranks against her.

As she hesitated indecisively, Emily and Don drew away from the others. At first they talked earnestly, but gradually an argument developed. Emily's defensive posture became more aggressive, judging by her pugnaciously lifted chin and the hands on her hips. What could Don have said to raise her dander? Emily was usually so submissive.

Their disagreement escalated, growing more heated until, with a final burst of anger, she stormed off. Don started after her, then changed his mind and stalked away in the other direction.

A case of thieves falling out? Sabena wondered if she'd achieved her goal inadvertently. Emily usually accepted Don's decisions with only minor grumbling. Had he finally pushed her too far?

Sabena was torn in two directions. Now was the time to question Emily, while she was too upset to be cautious. But it was equally important to find out what Jake had to say. She decided to wait. Emily wouldn't calm down that fast, considering the intensity of her quarrel with Don.

Sabena waited impatiently for Jake to finish with the Fabians. The conference—if anything so emotional could be called that—seemed to go on forever. All of the Fabians were outspoken at normal times; now they were unstoppable.

Eventually Jake called a halt. He silenced them with an imperiously raised hand and delivered a short speech. They grumbled, but the steam had been taken out of them. The sniping they did among themselves as they dispersed was mostly from habit.

Jake was smiling wryly when he rejoined Sabena. "I feel like a teacher in a school for delinquent children," he said.

"What was their explanation for being here?" Sabena asked.

"Marguerite's was the weirdest. She thought it would make an interesting incident if she ever wrote her memoirs."

So Pete's impression had been correct, Sabena mused. "How about Charles? Why was he doing that imitation of Groucho Marx?"

"He says he came along to protect his sister, after she told him she intended to keep the appointment."

"That seems rather thin. They don't even like each other."

Jake shrugged. "He might want to throttle her himself at times, but giving somebody else the pleasure is another thing entirely."

"I suppose so. That brings us to Harriet."

"The most practical one. She planned to get the man to say something incriminating so she could get the evidence on a tape recorder she had in her purse."

Sabena frowned. "She'd never have gotten away with it, but that doesn't clear her. She might have been trying to find out what he knew."

"I'm just making my report as promised," Jake answered.

"What happened between Emily and Don?"

"He was furious at the Fabians for being there. He said they'd scared the blackmailer away with their antics, ruining his chance to find out what the guy was up to. Then Harriet blew her stack and told him he was the one who had no business being there."

"She does have a point, although I realize Don's concern was for Emily," Sabena said.

"Emily wasn't impressed. She said the money wasn't worth all of this. She said she was ashamed of what it had done to them."

"That's practically an admission of guilt!" Sabena exclaimed.

"I think she was referring to their readiness to meet with a blackmailer."

"I don't agree. Don't you see? Emily and Don snatched Lucky, but now she's having second thoughts," Sabena said excitedly. "What was their argument about?"

"I don't know. They walked away a short distance and I couldn't hear what they were saying. The rest of the Fabians were all talking at once. As you must have noticed." He grinned. "When I finally got a word in, I sent them home and told them to behave themselves."

"You have to talk sense to Emily, too," Sabena said urgently. "Convince her to bring Lucky back, if he's still alive. She'll never get any pleasure out of the money, otherwise."

"I'm sure you're on the wrong track, Sabena."

She uttered a tiny sound of frustration. Why wouldn't Jake listen to her? She wasn't asking him to betray his client, only to urge Emily to do the right thing. But Jake couldn't care less about a cat. He might not be involved in the crime, but he condoned it.

Jake watched her broodingly for a moment. "All right, I'll talk to her if it will make you happy."

The constriction around Sabena's heart eased slightly. "I'd appreciate it," she said softly. "Even if it doesn't do any good."

He continued to stare at her, a torrent of emotions coursing across his strong face. When he spoke, it had nothing to do with the Fabians. "What happened to us, Sabena? I thought we were happy together."

She bowed her head as she remembered just how happy. "Things kept coming up," she murmured.

"And I know their names," he answered grimly. He tipped her chin up, forcing her to look at him. "We had too much going for us to let it end like this. Don't you agree?"

"I . . . I guess so."

"Would you be willing to start over?" He waited intently for her answer.

It was like a reprieve from a life sentence of loneliness. Stars shone in Sabena's eyes as she said, "I am, if you are."

Jake's smile lit up his entire face. "I'm more than willing. You might call me eager." He cupped her cheek in his palm. "I could spend a whole week telling you how much I've missed you in just one day."

"I won't ever get tired of hearing it," she whispered.

"If you keep looking at me like that, I'm going to make love to you right this minute," he said huskily.

She smiled. "I'd rather you picked a spot with less people."

"I know the perfect place. How would you like to fly to Paris for a week?"

"It sounds divine."

"That's what I hoped you'd say. I'll make reservations on the first flight out."

"You aren't serious?" she asked uncertainly.

"Of course I am. We need to get away alone together."

"But you're in the middle of a case. And so am I," she added.

"The world won't fall apart if we take a week off," he answered impatiently.

Sabena's happiness receded slowly. Why now, when she was so close to solving the Fabian case? Was Jake trying to lure her away so he could protect Emily? Sabena prayed that she was being unfair to him.

"Let's go next week, instead," she suggested artlessly. "That will give me time to get ready."

"How much time do you need? You can buy a complete wardrobe in Paris."

"I still have to make certain arrangements."

"Like what?"

"Well...stopping the newspaper and...well, a lot of things," she concluded lamely.

Jake gazed at her impassively. "You don't want to go, do you?"

"I do! I simply want to wait until next week."

"Why?"

"Why not?" she countered. "What's so special about *this* week?"

"I thought you wanted to be with me as much as I wanted to be with you," he answered evenly. "Evidently I was mistaken."

"Was that your real reason, Jake? Or were you simply interested in getting me far away from the Fabians?"

"Nobody puts anything over on *you*, do they, Sabena?" His eyes were frosty. "My concern for you was misplaced. You're as much of a street fighter as I am." He gave a bark of harsh laughter. "It's a wonder we didn't check each other for concealed weapons before we went to bed together."

Her cheeks blanched, but she kept her head high. "That's rather gross, but at least I'm glad you didn't refer to what we did as making love." She turned and walked away deliberately, giving no indication of the pain slicing through her like a knife.

Jake remained motionless. Even his eyes were lifeless.

Carey was waiting when Jake got back to the office. He could hardly contain his good news. "Wait till you hear what I pulled off, Chief. You're going to be really pleased.''

"Later," Jake said curtly, striding into his office.

Carey followed him inside. Ordinarily he would have been warned off by Jake's thunderous mood, but Carey thought he had a cure for it. "It's about the Fabian case."

"Naturally." Jake's voice dripped acid. "I used to have an engrossing law practice, but no more. The Fabians have taken over my entire life."

"Not for much longer," Carey said happily. "That's what I want to tell you. They could be out of your hair in a matter of days."

Jake's eyes narrowed. "What do you know that I don't?"

"I talked to Judge Weinstein's law clerk. Jerry Madison and I went to school together. He's a good guy and he owes me a favor. I used to loan him my notes when he missed a lecture—which was a fairly common occurrence." Carey laughed.

Jake gritted his teeth. "Would you get to the point?"

"Sure, I was just ... well, anyway, you know how crowded the court calendars are. It could take months to get a hearing on our plea to have the will set aside."

"I presume this is all leading up to something."

"You bet! Jerry is arranging for our case to be heard *this week!* Isn't that fantastic?"

Jake stared at him silently for a long moment. His voice was flat when he finally spoke. "If she had any lingering doubts, this will convince her."

Carey looked puzzled. "I don't understand. I thought you'd be pleased. I mean, you wanted everything to be over with, didn't you? I was only trying to help."

"You did the right thing. The Fabians should be very happy," Jake said somberly.

"Are you going to tell them right away, or wait till the hearing? I can't imagine anything could go wrong."

Jake's smile was a mere tic of facial muscles. "That's because you're young."

"The only thing that could upset the apple cart would be if Martha could produce Lucky," Carey argued. "But we both know she can't."

Jake sat up abruptly. "I have to call Martha. It isn't something I look forward to, but I don't want her to hear the news from one of the Fabians."

"Do you want me to phone her?" Carey asked.

"No. Why should you be the bad guy?" Jake's mouth curved sardonically. "I've had more practice at it."

Chapter Ten

Sabena forced herself to climb the steps of the Metropolitan Museum, although every movement was an effort. Why was she here, anyway? What difference did it make if Emily had committed a crime and gotten away with it? Nothing seemed important after her shattering encounter with Jake.

It wasn't Martha's fault, though. She'd also suffered at the hands of Jake the destroyer. Sabena couldn't quit on Martha just because her own life was in shambles. She squared her shoulders and proceeded with her original plan.

Emily was sitting motionless at her desk, staring down at a piece of paper as though she'd never seen one before.

Sabena pinned a smile on her face. "Hi. I was hoping I'd catch you in."

Emily looked up with a frown. "I'm sorry, but I'm busy, Sabena." Her manner was uncharacteristically curt.

"I don't blame you for being tired of me," Sabena said ruefully. "I keep popping up like a bad penny."

"Forgive me. I didn't mean to be rude." Emily sighed. "I've just had a rotten morning."

"Me, too. My wallet was stolen."

"What a shame! How did that happen?"

"I guess it was my own fault. I had my purse open on the counter while I was looking at some posters in the gift shop."

"Your wallet was stolen here in the museum? That's terrible!"

"Oh well, there wasn't much money in it, but replacing my credit cards will be a nuisance."

"Did you report the theft to the security guard?" Emily asked.

"It wouldn't do any good. Whoever took it is long gone. I stopped in to see you because I hoped you might loan me cab fare."

"Certainly." Emily took a bill from her purse. "Is that enough?"

"More than enough. Thanks. I'll pay you back tomorrow."

"There's no hurry. I'm just sorry it happened here."

"Don't be. Pickpockets are everywhere. It's sort of upsetting, though. You never expect it to happen to you."

"I know what you mean. Would you like a cup of coffee?"

Sabena had been angling for this kind of opportunity, but she said, "I don't want to take up any more of your time. You're busy."

"I'm not really. I was just wrestling with a personal problem."

"Maybe it would help to talk about it. Then I won't feel as if I'm imposing," Sabena added quickly.

"You aren't." Emily stood. "There's a coffee machine at the end of the hall. How do you take yours?"

"Black will be fine."

After Emily returned with two paper cups filled with coffee, they sat across from each other. "I hope this won't sour you on New York," she said.

"Not at all. It could happen anywhere," Sabena replied.

"You've been here quite a while," Emily commented. "It must be nice to get that much vacation time."

"I'm not really on vacation. I'm between jobs."

"I don't think you ever mentioned what it is you do."

"I'm a legal secretary." It was the first profession that occurred to Sabena.

"No wonder you and Jake hit it off so well."

Sabena glanced down at her cup to hide the pain of remembrance. "We don't get along all that well," she said in a low voice.

"You could have fooled me." Emily laughed.

"Jake is good at fooling everybody."

Emily's face sobered. "I'm beginning to think all men are. Do you ever really know them?"

"You must know Don pretty well." Sabena's taut body relaxed slightly. The conversation was finally going in the direction she was aiming at. "I envy you. You two seem so happy together."

Emily's laughter was harsh this time. "As long as I do everything he tells me to."

"You have to put your foot down if it's something you don't want to do," Sabena said casually.

"It isn't any one thing. It's his whole attitude."

"Toward what?"

Instead of answering the question, Emily asked abruptly, "How do you know if you really love someone?"

Sabena managed to keep her voice dispassionate. "In my opinion, there has to be more than physical attraction involved. You have to trust and respect the other person."

Emily didn't look any happier. "And how do you know if he loves *you?*"

Not by anything he says or does, Sabena could have told her. But this was no time to air her own troubles. "Are you and Don having problems?" she asked quietly.

"I'm beginning to realize we don't really agree on anything," Emily said slowly. "Don is a workaholic. All he cares about is getting ahead."

"You must have known that from the start," Sabena remarked.

"It was one of the things I admired about him. So many young men are confused about what they want to do with their lives. I was impressed by Don's drive."

"But now you're not?"

"I don't think money should become an obsession." Emily's face mirrored her distaste.

"That's a rather strong charge." Sabena worked hard to appear nonjudgmental. "What makes you think he's not simply ambitious?"

"I'm starting to wonder about a lot of things," Emily answered somberly. "Like whether Don would have asked me to marry him if I wasn't an heiress."

"You weren't when you two started to go together," Sabena had to point out.

"He knew I had prospects."

"It must have been very disappointing for him when Katherine's will was read."

"He was wild! At the time I thought it was on my behalf, but now I'm not so sure. Today he—"

When Emily didn't continue, Sabena prompted her. "What happened today?"

"We had an argument. Looking back, I realize it's the first time I ever stood up to him."

"What was the argument about?"

"He wanted me to go home and wait for—" Emily paused. "It isn't important."

Sabena let her breath out on a puff of frustration. "It is if you're this upset about it."

"I'm probably just having a case of premarital jitters." Emily tried to smile. "Don is pressing me to set the date."

"If you're having doubts, you'd better do something about them now," Sabena said urgently. "Jake indicated the will is going to be settled soon."

Emily sighed. "It will be a relief to have it all over with."

"For you, maybe. Martha will always be under a cloud."

"I'm truly sorry for her, but she shouldn't have tried to pass that other cat off as Lucky."

"You know she didn't." Anger edged Sabena's voice. "You even told me you didn't suspect Martha of any wrongdoing."

"I want to believe in her, but you have to admit appearances are against her. Why didn't she tell us Lucky was gone? Why did she wait until Jake took a second set of prints before admitting this was a different cat?"

"You got your money's worth when you hired Jake," Sabena said sarcastically. "Only someone with his suspicious mind would think of double-checking the cat."

"Actually, Don was the one who suggested it. Jake refused at first, but Don hates to back down. He took his idea to the family. They were so anxious to find a loophole in the will that they drove Jake crazy until he agreed. As it turned out, Don was right."

Sabena sat absolutely motionless, staring across the desk. Don wasn't familiar with Lucky. He hadn't been around him that often. What reason would he have for requesting a second set of prints? None, unless he knew they wouldn't match the first set.

Sabena finally knew who had abducted the cat. Only one question remained—besides the crucial one of Lucky's fate. Did Don act alone, or with Emily's knowledge and/or help?

Of more importance was the need to find Lucky quickly, or proof that Don had killed him. Sabena was chagrined to remember that she hadn't checked Don out as thoroughly as the others. Especially his apartment.

She pushed her chair back and rose. "I've taken up enough of your time. I'll let you get back to work."

Emily misunderstood her abruptness. "I wish you weren't angry at me. I never wanted Martha to get hurt."

"I guess she'll survive."

Emily was reluctant to let her leave. "I'll speak to Jake about giving her plenty of time to move. I doubt if the house will sell that fast, anyway."

Sabena paused at the door. "You've given up the idea of buying it yourself?"

"I spoke to Don about the possibility, and he was dead set against it. I guess I was being overly sentimental."

Sabena smiled sardonically. "That's a failing Don doesn't suffer from."

"You really dislike him, don't you?" Emily asked quietly.

"Your feelings are the only ones that matter." Sabena glanced at her watch. "I have something I have to do. It might make up your mind for you." She was hoping that Emily had been an innocent dupe. With any luck, the next hour should tell.

After leaving the museum, Sabena found a phone booth and called her answering service. She was eager to get to Don's apartment, but she'd been out of touch with her office for several hours. Most of the messages were routine, but the one from Martha sounded urgent.

"Has something come up?" she asked the older woman a few moments later.

"What I've been expecting," Martha replied. "Jake has succeeded in getting his plea on the court calendar. The case will be decided this week."

"I know."

"Jake already told you?"

"You might say that," Sabena answered bitterly. "I was certain the hearing was set for this week, but don't worry. I wasn't going to tell you until I had everything wrapped up, but I think I finally know who took Lucky."

"That's wonderful! Is he all right?"

"I don't know. I hope so, but even if he isn't, you'll be cleared."

"He simply has to be all right! Which one of them took him?"

"It wasn't one of the Fabians, after all. It was Don."

"Oh, dear! This will upset Emily terribly."

"She may have helped him. I don't have all the facts yet."

"Where is Lucky now? What are you doing about getting him back?"

"I'm hoping he's hidden in Don's apartment. I'm going over there as soon as I hang up."

"Isn't that dangerous?" Martha sounded apprehensive. "If he could do a disgraceful thing like that, there's no telling what he might do to keep from being found out."

"He doesn't know he has been. Don won't find out until he gets home tonight."

"Suppose he should come home early and surprise you?"

"That's the one thing I don't have to worry about. It would take blasting powder to get Don out of the office early. He and Jake are two of a kind," Sabena said grimly. "The client is the only one who counts."

"You don't still suspect Jake of being involved?"

"No. He figured out my blackmail scheme, but he didn't tell Don. That puts him in the clear."

"I don't understand," Martha said in bewilderment. "What's this about blackmail?"

"It isn't important. I have to go, Martha. If all goes well, I'll deliver Lucky to you shortly. Wish me luck."

"I have all my fingers crossed. But what happens if he isn't there?"

"I'll still find him, now that I know where to look. I'll reconstruct all of Don's movements since Lucky disappeared. It will take a little longer, but we'll get him."

"Maybe too late," Martha said soberly. "The hearing is at nine o'clock tomorrow morning."

"That can't be!"

"I'm afraid it is. Jake had the courtesy to phone and tell me himself. He said I was welcome to be there, but I didn't see the point in humiliating myself further. If the Fabians take my absence as a sign of guilt, what difference does it make? It isn't their opinion I'm worried about."

Sabena wasn't listening. She was shocked by how swiftly Jake had moved, although it shouldn't have surprised her. That was the reason he wanted to get her on the first plane out of town.

But she needed more time! It would be galling to fail now, with victory in sight. Perhaps she could convince Jake to ask for a postponement if she explained the circumstances. It was in his clients' best interests to clear up the mystery of Lucky's disappearance. They might lose out on the money entirely if Don got overconfident and killed the cat. The court could decide he was working for the family.

"Martha, I have to hang up. You'll be hearing from me soon."

"Be careful, Sabena. I'd never forgive myself if anything happened to you."

"It won't," Sabena answered confidently. "I'm on a roll."

Her bravado faded as she faced the prospect of talking to Jake once more. She dialed his number quickly before her courage failed.

Hearing his voice again was as disturbing as she'd known it would be. His tone wasn't as harsh as last time, but his mockery was almost worse.

"I didn't expect to hear from you again, Sabena. Was there something you forgot to accuse me of? Polluting the rivers? World hunger?"

She took a deep breath to steady herself. "I just spoke to Martha. She told me the hearing is scheduled for tomorrow morning."

"So now you know why I wanted to rush you out of town," he said ironically. "Okay, I'm listening. Tell me what an unprincipled heel I am, how I exploited you for my own gain. You *would* have gotten a trip to Paris out of it, though."

Her misery was compounded by his derision, but she forced herself to remain calm. "That's not why I called."

His voice was suddenly wary. "What trick do you have up your sleeve now?"

"No more tricks. I only want to ask you to postpone the hearing for a few days."

"You must be joking! Maybe you're enjoying this little cat-and-mouse game, but I'm not. I want you out of my hair and out of my life." Jake's pent-up anger erupted.

"We share a common goal, believe me! But I've discovered something that undermines your entire case. I know who took Lucky."

Jake swore under his breath. "You never give up, do you? I admire your determination, but I wish you'd use it where it will do some good. This case is over. Face it!"

"It isn't over," she insisted. "I'm offering you a chance to avoid making the biggest mistake of your life."

"You're too late," he answered grimly. "I've already made it."

"You're not the only one," she flared. "But at least I don't let personal feelings cloud my judgment. All I'm asking for is a postponement."

There was a short silence while Jake struggled with his temper. When he spoke, his voice held cold finality. "The subject is closed. I can't help you."

"All right, but you're going to look damn silly when I produce the cat and your clients have to give back the money. I'd like to be there when you try to get Harriet's share away from her."

"Are you serious?" Jake sounded a little less positive. "This isn't just a last-ditch effort to gain time?"

"Absolutely not! I might need a few days, but I can almost certainly guarantee results."

He was quick to catch her last-minute hedging. "That's what I thought. You're bluffing."

"Are you willing to take that chance? Remember what the newspapers did to Martha."

"Give me some reason to believe you," he said intently. "Who do you suspect of having taken Lucky?"

"You don't honestly think I'll tell you?"

"Okay, then tell me this. Is he still alive?"

"I don't know. I'm on my way to find out now."

"What have you gotten yourself into, Sabena?" he asked sharply. "If this is on the level, you could be in danger."

"It's funny the way you always get concerned about my safety when I start getting close to the truth," she said ironically.

"We can argue later. Right now, I want you to promise me you won't do anything foolish."

"I know exactly what I'm doing. You'll hear from me later today."

"Sabena, wait! Let me come with you."

"Oh, no! This is one time you're not going to gum up the works."

"I won't get in your way, I swear. I'll just be there in case you need me."

"I don't need you," she said firmly before hanging up.

"Tell me something I *don't* know," he muttered, staring moodily at the phone. A moment later he dialed Martha's number.

"What is it this time, Jake?" Martha asked wearily on hearing his voice.

"Sabena just called me with some wild story about having located Lucky."

"Why are you so sure it isn't true?" Martha asked coolly.

"I'm not. I want to know who she suspects."

"Why didn't you ask her?"

"I did, but she wouldn't tell me."

"Then *I* certainly won't. I'm not a complete fool, although you've all been treating me like one—or worse. You don't want Lucky to be found."

"That's not true. If there's been any skullduggery, I want to know about it."

"So you can exercise spin control?" Martha asked cynically.

"No! My God, you people think I have horns and a tail. I'm sworn to uphold the law, not break it."

"I'm disappointed in you, Jake, but I told Sabena right from the beginning that I didn't think you were involved."

"A fat lot of good that did," he muttered. "She never trusted me. Even after we—well, never mind. That's all over with."

"You two are interested in each other, aren't you?" Martha asked slowly.

"I'm afraid it was all one-sided, but that's not what matters now. I'm concerned about her safety. I have to know who she went to meet."

"She isn't meeting anyone."

Jake ran rigid fingers through his thick hair. "How can I convince you that I'm not the enemy? If that cat is alive, I'll gladly drop the petition. I'm not out to get you."

"I'm inclined to believe you, but I told you the truth. Sabena is going to...a place where she thinks Lucky is hidden. Nobody else will be there. At least I hope not." Martha couldn't hide her misgivings.

Jake groaned. "Suppose somebody is? Are you willing to take that chance?"

"She seemed so sure nothing would go wrong, but I'll admit I'm worried about her."

"Then *tell* me! While we're wasting time, Sabena could be walking into a trap."

"Oh, dear. She's at Don's apartment," Martha said hurriedly.

"Don Scudder? Emily's fiancé?" Jake sounded thunderstruck. "I always thought he was a jerk, but I didn't realize he was a fool, as well. What made Sabena suspect *him?*"

"I don't know, but she sounded very certain. Go after her, Jake. Don't let anything happen to her."

"I won't. Thanks for keeping an open mind, Martha. I could kiss you." He hung up and was out of his chair in one lithe movement.

At her end, Martha smiled. "Just invite me to the wedding."

The traffic on Fifth Avenue was horrendous. Sabena sat in the back seat of a cab, feeling her nerves jangling like castanets. She had plenty of time. Don wouldn't leave the office unless it burned down. Even then, he'd stick around to try to sell stocks to the firemen. But there were other problems with her plan. What she intended to do was flat-out illegal.

Biting her lip, Sabena leaned forward. "Maybe it would be faster if you went through the park."

"I gotta get there first, lady," the taxi driver said, with the consummate scorn that New York cabbies are famous for.

Sabena sat back and tried to relax as horns blared all around her and cars inched forward at a maddeningly slow pace.

Instead of feeling relief when she reached Don's apartment house, Sabena's tension mounted. This was the tricky part. She took the stairs instead of the elevator, keeping a lookout for the super. Luckily he was nowhere in sight.

Pausing at the door of Don's apartment, Sabena rang the bell, then knocked just to be sure. When there was no answer, she opened her purse and took out a long steel pick. A few deft movements unlocked the door and she slipped inside quickly.

Her pulse was racing as she surveyed the living room. It had a musty, closed-up smell and a deserted feeling. Don's personal fastidiousness didn't extend to his apartment. The windows needed washing, and the top of the television set was dusty. The room looked as though no one had used it for a long time. Could she be wrong?

As Sabena was about to continue her inspection, footsteps approached the front door. She froze, listening to the sound of someone attempting to turn the knob. Then the doorbell rang. Her heart resumed beating as she realized it couldn't be Don.

Not that her situation was improved. The stranger was creating such a disturbance that somebody was bound to investigate sooner or later. Not content with ringing the bell, he was banging on the door, as well. What if it was a delivery man? The super might come and let him in.

As Sabena was about to hide in a closet, a man's voice called, "Open up, Sabena. I know you're in there."

She recognized Jake's voice, even though it was muffled by the thick panel. Shock riveted her to the spot. Jake had fooled her even more completely than she thought. He *was* in conspiracy with Don. That was the only way he could know where to find her.

"Damn it, Sabena, you know I won't go away," he thundered. "Let me in."

She had no choice. If she didn't, one of the other tenants might call the police. Maybe she'd be safer with a police officer. How far was Jake prepared to go to keep her quiet? In spite of her apprehension, Sabena wasn't prepared to give up easily.

Setting her jaw, she flung open the door. "Why didn't you just ask Don for his key?"

Jake barely heard her. "Are you out of your mind, coming here alone?" he demanded. "Do you know what he'd do if he found you here?"

"What are *you* prepared to do? Offer me a deal?"

His eyes glittered with anger. "That would be like making a pact with the devil."

"It takes one to know one!" Sabena quaked inwardly as he advanced to tower over her, powerful and menacing. She stood her ground, however, throwing her head back to glare up at him.

"You are easily the most irritating, obstinate woman in the entire world," he rasped.

"You aren't high on my list of all-time favorites, either," she flared.

"At least I have sense enough not to break into somebody's apartment."

This was the part she was uncomfortable about. "How do you know I broke in? Maybe the door was open and I thought Don was at home."

Jake gave her a disgusted look. "Don't you realize he could have shot you and claimed he thought you were a burglar?"

"Is that why *you* came, instead? You draw the line at murder?"

"Okay, you win." He threw up his hands. "I'm the master criminal of the universe. I won a gold medal for kicking dogs and pinching helpless babies."

"You expect me to believe you had nothing to do with Lucky's disappearance? How else would you know exactly where to find me? All I told you was that I'd cracked the case. I didn't tell you who I suspected."

"Martha told me. I phoned her after you hung up on me."

"She wouldn't give you bus fare! Not after the way you've treated her."

"That's another misconception of yours. I never tried to hurt Martha. In spite of what you persist in believing, the story in the newspaper didn't come from me."

"You really didn't know Don took Lucky?" Sabena asked uncertainly.

"I honestly believed Martha had switched the cats— except for a brief period when I thought you were responsible." A glimmer of a smile softened his expression.

The tight band around Sabena's chest eased somewhat. "I'm glad you didn't do it, Jake."

"Are you sure Don did?" He looked around the living room. "I don't see any signs of a cat."

"I just got here. I haven't had a chance to search the apartment."

"You're going to get me disbarred yet," he said wryly.

"You don't have to stay. Go back to your office. I'll tell you if I find anything, I promise."

He ruffled her hair playfully. "Come on, let's get started. Maybe they'll put us in a coeducational prison."

"Is there such a thing?" Sabena felt suddenly lighthearted. This was the Jake she remembered—and still loved.

"Not in this country, so we'd better not get caught. Where do you want to look?"

"Everywhere. It shouldn't take long. It's only a small apartment." Sabena started for the kitchen with Jake following.

There was a cup and saucer in the sink, but other than that, this room was as unused-looking as the living room. No notes were stuck to the refrigerator, no newspapers or magazines littered the counter.

"He doesn't appear to spend much time here," Jake commented, glancing around. "Although, I can't say I blame him. This is a really dreary place."

"It has Don's personality," Sabena observed tartly.

"Are you certain you're on the right track? Lucky was supposed to be very friendly. Wouldn't he have come out to greet us by now?"

"If he was able to." She didn't want to think of what Don might have done to the poor cat.

Sabena looked under the sink without finding anything significant. The wastebasket held a few crumpled paper towels and some discarded envelopes. She fished those out gingerly, but they were from the utility company and a couple of department stores, ordinary monthly bills.

She opened cupboard doors with mounting disappointment. The evidence against Don had been so conclusive. But one cabinet held glasses and dishes, another canned goods. What you'd expect to find in anybody's kitchen.

Jake was helping her search, with the same lack of success. "Why are we doing this? Even Don wouldn't keep a cat stashed in among the groceries."

"I'm looking for cat food—and I found it!" Sabena grabbed a bag off a shelf and turned to Jake with shining eyes. "Look! I was right!"

"I hate to puncture your balloon, but it doesn't really prove anything. He could have owned a cat at one time, or maybe he likes to feed strays."

"*Don?*"

"I'll admit it's unlikely, but where's Lucky?"

"We haven't looked in the bedroom yet. Oh, Jake, I hope he hasn't killed him."

Jake took her hand and squeezed it hard. "If he did, it will be the sorriest day of his life."

The bedroom showed signs of its owner. Slippers had been kicked off beside the bed, and an indentation on the coverlet indicated where Don had sat down to put on his shoes.

The adjoining bathroom had towels hung haphazardly over rods. An electric razor was still plugged into an outlet beside the mirror over the sink, and the bath mat was scrunched up. Everything looked normal. There was no sign of a cat.

Sabena sighed. "Either Don disposed of Lucky, or he has him hidden somewhere else."

"Is it possible that you've made a mistake?" Jake asked gently. "I don't like the guy, either, but having an abrasive personality doesn't make him a criminal."

Her shoulders sagged. "I was so sure."

"Tell me what made you suspect Don."

She related her conversation with Emily. "All this time I thought paw-printing the cat was your idea, but she said the second test was Don's."

"The first one was, too," Jake said thoughtfully. "It was an excellent suggestion, so I acted on it. I was annoyed when he wanted to do it all over again, but I didn't attach any importance to his insistence. I simply wrote it off as Don's tendency to try to make himself important."

"Being a jerk worked to his advantage," Sabena said ruefully. "You do believe me now, don't you?"

"Yes, but it might be too late. Carey was so proud of himself for getting the hearing moved up that he phoned all the Fabians."

"*Carey* was responsible for that?"

Jake's eyes held hers, but all he did was nod.

Sabena looked away, remembering her terrible accusations and the resultant bitterness on both sides. She also had a flashback to the pain on Jake's face. Why hadn't she noticed it at the time? Because she was too busy jumping to conclusions, Sabena thought bitterly. And now it was too late. How could Jake ever forgive her? He was here now because he was a decent person and he didn't want her to get hurt, but she'd killed any deeper feelings he'd had for her.

"I hate to say this." Jake interrupted her pointless remorse. "But if Emily phoned Don and told him about the hearing, he might have felt confident enough to dispose of Lucky."

Sabena pushed her own troubles aside in the urgency of the moment. "Anything's possible, but he would have had to leave work, come home to do the job, then find somewhere to dump him. Since Don couldn't know there was any urgency, why not wait until tomorrow, or even the weekend?"

"That's true," Jake agreed. "But the cat's days are clearly numbered unless we find out where Don is keeping him."

"You know him better than I do. Have you any idea where that might be?"

"We aren't exactly buddies. I've avoided him as much as possible."

"He must have dropped some small clue. Anything you can remember will help. Think hard."

As they gazed at each other in deep concentration, a tiny noise broke the stillness. It sounded almost like a baby crying. They continued to stare at each other for a moment, this time in disbelief.

Sabena broke the spell. "The closet!" she shouted. "We didn't get around to looking in there."

The only closet in the room was the old-fashioned kind that extended inside, almost the length of the wall. It was long, but inconvenient. Garments hung at the far end were almost inaccessible. To reach them, a person would have had to actually wriggle inside, past the hanging garments up front.

Jake found an easier way. Yanking armloads of suits and jackets off the rod, he threw them on the bedroom floor. At the extreme end of the dark closet, pushed up against the wall, was an overturned wooden crate. As they made their way toward it, the tiny sound was repeated.

Jake lifted the crate and hurled it aside. Underneath was an emaciated black cat, too weak to stand up. All he could do was look at them out of huge, dull eyes, and mew piteously.

Sabena was down on her knees in an instant, gathering the little creature in her arms while making crooning sounds of reassurance.

Jake glared down at them, swearing pungently. He aimed a kick at an empty dish on the floor, shattering it against the wall. "He doesn't even have any water!"

"At least he's alive." Sabena stood with the cat in her arms and carried him into the bedroom.

"Barely," Jake growled.

The bright light revealed Lucky's desperate condition. His fur was matted and he remained limp in Sabena's arms.

"He's nothing but skin and bones," she exclaimed.

"God knows when he was fed last. We have to get him to a vet immediately."

"Oh, Jake! He just closed his eyes."

"It's probably the bright light after all that time in a dark, airless closet. Find something to wrap him in while I look for a telephone book."

Sabena opened dresser drawers until she found one containing sweaters. She pulled out the top one and threw it on the bed. Gently placing the cat in the middle, she wrapped him up like a baby in a blanket.

Jake returned with a sheet of paper he'd ripped from the Yellow Pages. "There's a vet not too far from here. Let's go."

Sabena smiled faintly as she followed him to the door. "This is one of Don's cashmere sweaters. Can't you just imagine what he'd say if he knew!"

"He'd better hope this cat survives, or he'll have to practice talking without his front teeth," Jake said grimly.

Chapter Eleven

The veterinarian was young and competent, but not very encouraging. "What the devil happened to this cat?" he asked.

"He was closed up in a closet for weeks," Sabena answered without going into details.

"They can get into the darndest places. This one used up almost all of his nine lives."

"He'll recover, though, won't he, Doctor?" she asked anxiously.

"I'll do my best, but I can't promise anything. He's dehydrated and he's suffering the effects of starvation. I've never seen a cat in worse shape."

Jake's face darkened. "What are his chances?"

"I'll know better after I make a more thorough examination." The doctor started for the door. "I'll be right back."

Jake approached the examining table and stroked the cat's head gently. "Hang in there, fella." When Lucky twitched his tail ever so slightly, Jake said, "That's the spirit. You're going to make it."

Sabena watched with growing wonder. She'd thought Jake's anger at Don was because of the Fabians. If Lucky died, the estate could be tied up in litigation for years. But Jake was acting as though Lucky was all that mattered. She'd never seen this gentle, caring side of Jake.

The doctor returned with an orderly and a bag full of instruments. "Why don't you go out to the waiting room now? Unless you'd rather phone me later for a report."

"We'll wait." Sabena knew instinctively that she was speaking for Jake, too.

Jake paced the waiting room, his face stormy. "I can't believe anyone could be that cruel to a defenseless animal!"

"I'm sure Emily couldn't," Sabena said. "I thought perhaps she and Don were in it together, but I've changed my mind. I can't imagine her allowing him to torture Lucky."

"Perhaps she didn't know about it. Don might have suggested keeping him at his house because there would be less chance of being found out."

Sabena shook her head. "Emily is fond of that cat. She would have visited him to make sure he was all right. I wonder how Don kept her out of his apartment all this time?"

"Any excuse would do. She'd believe the sun rises at midnight if he told her so," Jake said disgustedly. "He has her thoroughly brainwashed."

"Don't be too sure. Emily is naive, but she's not stupid. Let's see what she does when she finds out about Don."

"That reminds me. I have a call to make." Jake walked over to a high counter and spoke to the receptionist sitting at a desk on the other side. "Where can I find a public telephone?"

"You can use our phone if you like." She placed the instrument on the counter.

He dialed his office number and asked for his associate. When Carey answered, Jake said, "Drop whatever you're working on. I want you to get in touch with the Fabians immediately—all four of them. I don't care if you have to run down Marguerite at her beauty shop, or Charles at the racetrack. Just find them."

"Sure, Chief. Is anything wrong?" Carey asked uncertainly.

"I'll fill you in later. Tell them all to be at the Fabian house at five o'clock. I'll meet them there."

"What do I say when they ask why?"

"Tell them all the problems over the estate have been ironed out." Jake turned to smile sardonically at Sabena.

"But the hearing isn't until tomorrow."

"Just do as I say. And one more thing. Have Emily relay my message to Don. I want him there, as well."

After a moment of silence, Carey said, "I'll get right on it. Anything else?"

"No, that should cover it."

"You don't need me there, do you?" Carey asked.

"I think you should come. You might find it interesting."

"I might find skydiving interesting, too, but some-body would have to push me out of a plane first," Carey answered succinctly.

Jake chuckled. "This won't be nearly as traumatic. Round up the Fabians and meet me at five o'clock."

"I have to use the phone, too," Sabena said before he could return it. Her expression was troubled as she joined him at the counter. "Was it wise to alert Don? You've given him a couple of hours to clear away all traces of Lucky in his apartment. He'll deny every-thing, and it will be our word against his."

"You should be able to dig up enough evidence to tie him to the crime."

"I'm sure I can. For starters, I know I can locate the locksmith, given a little time. But Don is such a slippery character. I'd hate to see him bluff his way out of this somehow. I want to make him pay."

"Losing Emily and the money is probably the worst thing that could happen to him."

"We don't know for sure that she'll dump him. He's very successful at sweet-talking her."

"You were the one who said Emily wasn't stupid."

"Yes, but love does funny things to a woman."

"It makes her more trusting?" Jake asked with a flat inflection. "That's good to know."

Sabena looked away hurriedly, feeling her cheeks flush. "Even if Don does lose her, he deserves more punishment than that."

"Don't worry, he'll get it. I have a whole bag of in-dictments to suggest to the district attorney—stealing, conspiracy to commit fraud, illegal entry." Jake smiled. "Although perhaps I'd better not bring up that one."

"You never cease to surprise me," she said slowly.

"Why is that?"

"We had such arguments over Katherine's will. You said leaving that much money to a cat was absurd."

"Wouldn't you say I'd been vindicated? Look how things turned out."

"You couldn't foresee what happened."

"It was still a foolish act. Katherine could have taken care of her cat without resorting to such drastic measures. It was a foolishly sentimental gesture."

Before Sabena had gained insight into Jake's true character, she would have lashed out at him for his apparently callous viewpoint. Now, she merely smiled. "You don't believe in sentiment?"

"There's no room for it when millions of dollars are at stake."

"You're a fraud, Jake. You weren't thinking about the money when we found Lucky, more dead than alive."

"Naturally I was repelled. I'm not a monster. But it doesn't change my opinion."

"Why won't you admit you have feelings like the rest of us?" Sabena demanded. "That you're capable of being touched, of needing someone."

He stared at her, struggling with powerful emotions. Then his expression became remote. "I've learned the hard way not to expect anything from anybody."

Sabena was overcome by a feeling of hopelessness. Jake would never forgive her for not trusting him. She'd thrown away any chance she might have had of winning his confidence. He would be more wary than ever from now on. Especially of her.

"I have to call Martha," she said tonelessly.

The older woman answered on the first ring, as though she'd been waiting by the telephone. "I thought you'd never call!"

"This is the first chance I've had," Sabena explained.

"Did you find Lucky?" Martha asked anxiously.

"Yes. We found him." Sabena wasn't looking forward to telling her in what condition.

"That's wonderful!" Martha was happily unaware. "I never in a million years would have suspected Don, although I must admit I've never cared for him."

"He's a despicable person," Sabena said with distaste.

"Maybe now Emily will come to her senses. I'm awfully afraid he's only interested in her money."

"I've always thought that."

"Knowing what Don was capable of, I was very uneasy about letting you go to his apartment alone. That's why I told Jake where you were. That was all right, wasn't it?"

"As it turned out, I'm glad he was there," Sabena admitted.

"I thought you might be," Martha answered with a smile in her voice. "He's a good man to have around."

Sabena changed the subject abruptly. "We have to talk about Lucky, Martha."

"I can't wait to see him. How long will it take you to get here?"

"Well, the thing is . . . I can't exactly bring him to you right now."

"He's alive, isn't he?" Martha asked sharply.

"At the moment he is. I hate to have to tell you this, but Lucky was in very bad shape when we found him. Don kept him locked up without food or water for long periods of time. I wish there was some way to soften the blow, but you have to be prepared in case Lucky doesn't survive."

"Oh no," Martha whispered. "The poor little animal. How could anyone be so heartless?"

"I don't know," Sabena replied helplessly.

"Where is Lucky now? I want to see him."

"That might help." Sabena gave her the veterinarian's address. After cradling the receiver, she said to Jake, "Martha is coming right over. I hope Lucky hangs on until she gets here."

"He will. He's a scrappy little cat."

"What happens if he does die? To the money, I mean."

"That's hard to say. There are so many factors to take into account. One thing I can predict—it would be a long, drawn-out battle."

"What do you plan to tell the Fabians this afternoon?"

"Stick around and find out." Jake grinned. "I'm finally going to enjoy a meeting with them."

When the veterinarian opened the inner door a short time later, they turned to him eagerly. Sabena spoke for both of them. "Is he going to live, Doctor?"

"I can't give you a guarantee, but I'm almost positive he'll pull through. That's one tough little cat."

"I told you!" Jake put an arm around Sabena's shoulders and hugged her against him.

"Not very many animals would have survived what he went through, but his heartbeat is strong and he seems more alert since we started the intravenous. He was too weak to eat."

The bell over the outside door jangled and Martha came rushing in. After the doctor had repeated his prognosis, her anxiety faded somewhat.

"May I see him?" she asked.

"Certainly, but don't be upset by all the tubes."

"We're just happy to see him under *any* circumstances," Martha assured him.

Lucky did indeed look terrible, but his eyes weren't as glazed. When he saw Martha, he twitched his tail and even managed a muted meow.

"Poor dear little Lucky." Martha had tears in her eyes as she stroked him ever so gently. "How can I ever make it up to you?"

"Try smoked salmon and caviar for dinner." Jake laughed.

"I wouldn't mind being invited for that, myself," the veterinarian joked.

"You're all invited," Martha said. "When Lucky recovers, we'll have the granddaddy of all parties."

"You don't know it yet, but you're having a little gathering this afternoon," Jake told her. "I asked the Fabians and Don to meet me at your house at five."

Martha's mouth tightened into a thin line. "I've always considered myself a civilized person, but I can't guarantee what I might do to that man."

"You'll have to wait till *I* get through with him," Jake said.

The Fabians arrived on time and in a gala mood. Carey also showed up as he'd been told to, but his mood was in sharp contrast to theirs. He nodded to Jake, then stood by the door with his arms folded, not greeting anyone else.

After waiting in vain for him to join her, Emily walked over to him. "Aren't you going to say hello?" she asked.

"Hello," he answered ungraciously.

She looked hurt. "Are you angry with me, Carey?"

"No, of course not." His expression softened as he gazed at her lovely face. "I guess I'm just in a lousy mood, but that's no reason to take it out on you."

"I'm glad you're not angry," she said softly. "I'd hate to lose a friend."

His expression hardened once more and he glanced around. "Where's your fiancé?"

"Don was held up at the office." She sighed. "That's the story of my life."

"Why do you put up with it? If you were *my* fiancée, you'd come first."

Emily's lashes feathered her cheeks. "The girl who gets you will be very fortunate."

"I don't suppose there's any chance that *you'd* like to be that fortunate one." His light tone was meant to show he was joking, but they both knew he wasn't.

"I think there's a law against having two fiancés." Emily tried to smile, without much success.

"If there isn't, there should be." Carey's attempt to joke fell just as flat.

Emily changed the subject. "Do you know why Jake asked us all here today?"

"He didn't tell me, but the hearing is set for tomorrow. I suppose it has something to do with that."

"Well then, I guess it's almost over." She sighed.

"I guess so."

"I don't suppose we'll ever see each other again."

"Probably not." He slanted a glance at her. "Unless you're still interested in working out a plan to buy this house."

"Don is against the idea," she answered reluctantly.

"I see. Well, I suppose this is it, then," Carey said heavily. "Excuse me, I have to speak to Jake."

Jake was under siege by the Fabians. They were all crowded around, peppering him with questions.

"When can we expect to get our money?" Charles asked. "I don't like to rush you, but I have a few little financial obligations I'd like to clear up."

"And I want to leave for Europe," Marguerite said. "I've missed almost the entire social season waiting for this matter to be settled."

"I hope you aren't going to drag out the proceedings so you can pad your fee," Harriet said.

Sabena tried and failed to stifle her snort of laughter. She was standing just outside the family circle.

Harriet turned around and glared at her. "What's *she* doing here?"

"I asked her to come. Miss Murphy is almost solely responsible for the outcome of this case," Jake said smoothly.

"Thanks a lot," Sabena murmured to him in an aside.

"Why should I have all the fun?" He grinned.

"Can we get started?" Marguerite asked impatiently.

"I'm waiting for Don," Jake said.

"Why?" Harriet scowled. "He isn't family."

"He's taken an intense interest in the family fortunes," Jake answered dryly.

"Then why isn't he here? We're always waiting for someone," Harriet said querulously.

Jake looked at his watch, then called over to Emily, "You did give my message to Don, didn't you?"

"Yes, and he said he'd be here without fail, but he had something to do first."

Sabena shot Jake a worried glance. "You don't think he went home to feed Lucky?" she whispered.

"It was never a priority before."

"I swear, if he makes a run for it, I'm going to devote my career to tracking him down," Sabena declared angrily.

"Count me in," Jake told her.

The tension in the room was palpable. Everybody was experiencing high emotion of one kind or another. When Don finally showed up, he was the center of attention.

"It's about time," Charles said.

"Really, Donald, this is most inconsiderate of you," Marguerite sniffed.

"*I* don't know why we had to wait for him in the first place," Harriet said impatiently.

"Whoa, wait a minute!" Don held up both hands. "What's the big deal?" He glanced over at Emily. "Didn't you tell them I had a late appointment?"

"You didn't tell me *what* you were doing," she answered coolly.

"Don't start in on me again," he grated. "I had enough of that this afternoon."

Carey started toward him, but Jake put his hand on Carey's arm. "Will everyone please take a seat? Since you're all present now, I'll tell you why I called you together."

"Don't drag it out," Harriet said. "Just tell us when we can expect to get our money."

"You're the one who won't ever let the man finish a sentence," Charles said in annoyance. "You always have to be in charge of everything."

"Will you two stop bickering?" Marguerite asked.

Jake folded his arms over his chest. "I can wait," he said calmly.

"Do get on with it, Jake," Marguerite pleaded. "I can't stand the suspense another second. When do we get the money?"

"To answer your question directly—you don't."

They all stared at him blankly for an instant. "You're joking, aren't you?" Marguerite faltered.

"No, I'm quite serious."

"You can't do this to us," Charles sputtered. "I was counting on my share."

"That was a mistake."

Jake's matter-of-fact tone convinced them. As realization sank in, pandemonium broke loose. He was pelted from all sides by anger and recriminations.

Harriet took the lead, as usual. "You bled us dry and now you have the nerve to tell us we're not going to get anything for our money? How much did Martha pay you to double-cross us?"

"That's a rather serious accusation," he said mildly.

"Jake wouldn't do a thing like that. There must be some mistake." Marguerite turned to him with an anxious expression. "You mean, we'll simply have to be patient a little longer. That's right, isn't it?"

"I'm afraid not."

"But what's going to happen to the estate?" Charles asked. "We're Katherine's heirs. We're entitled to it!"

"And you'll get it—eventually."

"You see? I told you it was all a misunderstanding." Marguerite was limp with relief.

"You were playing a joke on us?" Harriet asked in outrage.

"I don't think that's very professional, old boy," Charles said stiffly.

Martha spoke up for the first time. "You people are a disgrace! You don't deserve one cent of Katherine's money. You never cared about her. It would serve you right if Lucky died."

"You're scarcely in a position to bring up that wretched cat," Marguerite told her acerbically.

"That's right." Harriet agreed with her sister in a rare instance. "You knew he'd run away, and you tried to cover up your criminal negligence at our expense."

Don had stayed in the background. Now he came forward to confront Jake. "What are you trying to pull, Waring? First you say we're not going to get the money, and then you say we are. Which is it?"

Jake's eyes were as hard as marbles. "I don't remember you being mentioned in the will."

Don waved a hand impatiently. "Emily and I will be married soon. That makes me a beneficiary the same as the others."

"Not if she has you sign a premarital agreement relinquishing all rights to her inheritance. Which is what I'd strongly advise her to do."

Don's handsome face turned ugly. "You have no right to mix into our affairs."

"No," Jake admitted. "It was an unsolicited piece of advice."

"We don't need your advice," Don said roughly.

"It's academic, in any case," Jake drawled. "I doubt if you'll be willing to wait an indeterminate number of years to get your hands on her money. That's supposing she still wants to marry you when you get out of jail."

"What the devil are you talking about?"

Jake's insouciance disappeared and his pent-up anger burst forth. "You miserable excuse for a human being! I'd like to beat your brains out—but I'd have to find them first. You didn't have to torture the cat."

"You're accusing *me* of having something to do with his disappearance? That's the stupidest thing I ever heard of. We all know Martha was responsible."

"That's what you wanted us to think, and you almost got away with it," Jake said grimly.

"You're out of your mind. This place is a fortress. I couldn't have gotten in even if I'd wanted to."

"You didn't have to get into the house. You took him out of the backyard. That's still a criminal act. Grand larceny, I'd say, considering his worth."

"Stop blowing smoke in my ear. You know as well as I do that the gate is always locked. How could I get into the backyard?"

Sabena couldn't restrain herself any longer. "You made an impression of the key. It's always kept on a peg in the kitchen."

Don turned on her furiously, beginning to look harried. "What the hell do you know about anything? You have no right to be here in the first place."

"Sabena is a private investigator," Martha said. "I hired her to find out what happened to Lucky."

"A private detective!" Charles gasped.

The older Fabians looked shocked. They'd followed the exchange between Jake and Don with varying degrees of disbelief and bewilderment.

Emily's face was deeply troubled. "None of this is true, is it, Don?" she asked.

"Of course not, sugarbabe. You know me better than that. Jake bungled the case, and now he's trying to make me the scapegoat. Any decent attorney would have gotten us the money by now."

"You haven't let me come to your apartment lately," she remarked hesitantly. "Every time I suggested it, you made some excuse."

"You know I don't like staying home. I spend as little time as possible in that dump of mine."

"Too bad you couldn't have stopped by once in a while to feed the cat." Jake's voice was wintry. "That's the part I can't forgive. It's no thanks to you that he isn't dead. We found him just in time."

Don's face was ashen as he darted a glance at Emily. He licked his dry lips. "Don't you see what he's doing? Jake picked me to be the fall guy. If he found that cat in my closet, somebody planted him there. I don't know anything about it."

"I didn't mention where I found him," Jake said.

"Well, I just assumed...I mean, where else would I— would anybody hide something?" Don was stammering and sweat stood out on his forehead.

Emily stared at him in horror. Guilt was written all over him. "How could you do such a despicable thing?" she whispered.

"Why are you taking Jake's word over mine?" Don tried to stem the tide flowing against him. "He doesn't have a shred of proof. He hasn't even produced the damn cat."

"Lucky is in a pet hospital," Jake said. "And you'd better pray he recovers."

"Was he that badly mistreated?" Emily asked apprehensively.

"I'm glad you didn't see him," Martha told her. "It would have broken your heart."

"They're making it sound worse than it is." Don had given up trying to deny his guilt. All he could do now was seek to minimize it. "So I couldn't get home to feed him a couple of times. Big deal!"

Emily gazed at him searchingly. "Did the money mean *that* much to you?"

"Hey, I did it for you, sugarbabe."

She continued to stare at him, as though seeing him for the first time. "You never loved me. You didn't even notice me until you found out Katherine Fabian was my aunt."

"You're wrong! I'm crazy about you," he said urgently. "Okay, so maybe I cut a few corners, but it was for you—for *us*. Can't you understand that?"

Sabena held her breath as Emily said, "I'm beginning to. You've had a slight change of plan. We won't get the money immediately, but perhaps I can borrow against my inheritance and you can still invest in your deal."

"That's right," he said eagerly. "We'll be living on easy street. We'll have everything we've always wanted."

She shook her head slowly. "We've never wanted the same things out of life. I think I've realized that for a long time, but I wouldn't admit I'd made a mistake." She slipped the engagement ring off her finger. "Goodbye, Don."

"You're going to regret this," he warned. "If I walk out that door, I'm not coming back."

Carey stepped forward before Emily could have second thoughts. "The lady made herself perfectly clear. If you need help finding the door, I'll be happy to assist you."

Don eyed the other man's more athletic build. Behind him was Jake, an even greater threat. "Don't strain yourself. I'm leaving. You couldn't pay me to stay here," Don snarled.

"Somehow, I doubt that," Jake drawled.

The others had remained mute during the dramatic revelations, like spectators at a gripping play. Even Harriet was speechless. With Don's departure, the spell was broken and the clamor began again. Emily didn't take part. She slumped into a chair, staring at her hands in her lap.

Carey got down on one knee beside her chair. "I'm sorry," he said simply.

"It was my own fault. I kept telling myself Don was ambitious, not greedy. That he was only watching out for my interests. He said so often enough! The rest of you could see him for what he was. Why couldn't I?"

"Love doesn't do a lot for your perception," Carey answered wryly.

"What I felt for Don wasn't love. I know that now. If it had been, I wouldn't have found excuses to put off our wedding. He kept urging me to set a date, but the idea scared me. Don was so . . . pretentious. I didn't want to spend the rest of my days with someone who couldn't enjoy the simple pleasures of life."

"Like a hamburger and a movie?" Carey asked softly.

"Exactly. You made me see what a relationship between a man and a woman should be like. Not that we had a relationship," she added hastily. "I realize you were only being a friend."

"You must have known it was more than that," he said deeply.

"I hoped it was," she murmured. "That was another reason for my reluctance to marry Don. I enjoyed being with you more than him. It made me feel guilty."

Carey gripped her hands in his. "This is probably a rotten time to tell you, but I'm in love with you, Emily."

A smile lit up her entire face. "Your timing couldn't be any better, I'm in love with you, too, Carey."

Her declaration didn't delight him the way it should have. "I'd like to think that's true," he said carefully. "But you're in a highly emotional state right now. Don let you down, and maybe you're simply turning to me for comfort.''

"Don't try to talk me out of it," she teased. "Maybe this will convince you." Framing his face between her palms, she kissed him.

Carey's response was instantaneous. Gathering her into his arms, he returned her kiss passionately. They were lost in the wonder of their discovery, oblivious to the others in the room. Which didn't matter. The only one who noticed was Sabena, and she approved thoroughly.

Carey finally relinquished Emily's mouth, but he kept his arms around her. "As long as I'm down on one knee, it seems like the right moment to propose." He drew back to gaze at her adoringly. "You don't have to give me an answer this minute. I know you'll need time to think about it."

She smiled ecstatically. "My mind is already made up. This time I don't have a single doubt. I'll marry you tomorrow if you like."

The tender way they looked at each other reminded Sabena of her own loss. Jake had looked at *her* that way once. Suddenly she needed to get away from this house, these people, everything that tied her to Jake. The case was over, and in time she'd forget him. Maybe in an eternity or two.

Sabena wanted to tell Martha she was leaving, but the older woman was standing in the group surrounding Jake. Sabena tried to get her attention, but she got Jake's, instead. He smiled and reached out for her hand, pulling her over to stand next to him. Sabena found herself clinging to his hand, powerless to let go. This was the last physical contact she'd ever have with him.

Jake rubbed his thumb absently over her knuckles, his attention on the Fabians. They were demanding to know what was going to happen next.

"First, you all owe Martha an apology," he said sternly. "I don't want to hear of any of you giving her a hard time, or you'll answer to me. Get on with your lives and forget about your sister's money. Just consider it an annuity that will mature at some future date."

After a lot of grumbling and hand-wringing, the elder Fabians eventually departed. Emily remained behind, looking radiant.

"I'm sorry for all the trouble we caused you, Martha," she said.

"You weren't responsible," Martha answered. "I never blamed you."

"I'm glad, because I'd like to continue to visit you and Lucky. This place is like home to me."

Carey put his arm around her shoulders. "Perhaps it will be someday. By the time Lucky goes to his well-earned reward in cat heaven, we might be able to swing it."

Emily laughed self-consciously. "In case you hadn't noticed, Carey and I...have become very good friends."

He chuckled. "If you tell it like it is, Jake might give me a raise. Emily and I intend to get married."

"I'm so happy for both of you." Martha looked at them speculatively. "Have you decided where you're going to live?"

"We just discovered we love each other," Emily protested, smiling at Carey.

"I think we should have a little talk," Martha said with satisfaction. "Sit down, both of you."

"They don't need us," Jake told Sabena.

"You're right." Sabena hugged Emily. "Goodbye and good luck."

"That sounds so final," Emily objected. "We'll see each other again."

"I hope so," Sabena answered noncommittally.

When they were outside, Sabena psyched herself up to say goodbye to Jake, also, but he spoke first. "Let's walk. I feel the need of some exercise after that donnybrook in there."

"It was pretty hectic," she agreed. Totally against her will, Sabena found herself walking down Park Avenue next to Jake.

"I'm glad Emily saw the light," he remarked. "She and Carey are certainly better suited to each other."

"It was really fortunate that he was around to pick up the pieces today. They might not have discovered how they felt about each other. At least, not this fast."

Jake grinned. "Carey really dragged his feet about coming, but I had a hunch it would work out this way."

"I can't imagine you in the role of matchmaker," Sabena commented. "You're the one who believes that marriage results in short haircuts."

Jake shrugged. "Some men are the marrying kind. Carey might as well marry the right girl."

Sabena hid her unhappiness. "It's ending like a fairy tale," she said lightly. "Everybody is going to live happily ever after."

"Katherine's brother and sisters might not agree with you." Jake laughed.

"I was referring to the people who really deserve a happy ending. Martha's name has been cleared and she found a caretaker for Lucky, someone who really loves him. That's what she's talking to Emily and Carey about. They'll be thrilled to live in the house, and Martha can move to the country the way she planned. It's the perfect solution."

Sabena hadn't noticed, but they'd been walking in the direction of Jake's apartment house. He stopped at the entrance.

"Would you like to come up for a drink?" he asked her.

"No thanks, I've had as much stimulation as I can take," she joked wryly.

"A cup of coffee, then. Decaf." Before she could refuse, Jake took her by the elbow and led her into the lobby.

"I really want to go home," she protested weakly.

"You need to unwind," he said soothingly.

She did, but that was impossible around Jake. Every nerve in her body was screaming as she followed him into his apartment. Sabena knew immediately that coming there was mistake. She couldn't continue to keep up appearances.

"Make yourself comfortable while I put the coffee on," he said.

"I really can't stay, Jake," she mumbled, turning back to the door.

"Too many memories?" he asked quietly. "Imagine how I feel, having to live here."

"Please don't. Just let me go while we can still part on good terms," she pleaded, turning to face him. "If I stay, we'll only wind up saying hurtful things to each other."

"That's certainly been the pattern." He stared at her

moodily. "So, why don't I just let you walk out the door and out of my life?"

"I was never part of your life," she said sadly. "You built a wall around yourself that I could never break through."

"How badly did you want to?"

"You see? We're on our way to another quarrel." She turned away.

Jake turned her around to face him, keeping his hands on her shoulders. "We're going to have this out once and for all. Did I ever mean anything to you?"

"What difference does it make now?" Sabena's control was slipping. If only he wouldn't touch her! His strong hands on her shoulders reminded her of happier times. "You never wanted more than an exciting affair. Well, that's what we had."

The abject misery on her face brought a dawning excitement to his. Jake's tight grip loosened and his hands became subtly caressing. "It doesn't have to be over. Since our physical relationship is so satisfying, why not continue to see each other?"

"No! I can't!"

She tried to twist away, but Jake's arms circled her waist, drawing her close. "Why not, Sabena?" he asked softly. "We still want each other."

"No, I . . . I don't." Her body was taut with the effort to resist his potent allure.

"I could prove you're wrong." His hand skimmed her breast seductively while his lips brushed over hers. "Remember the way it was? Those nights we made love in the moonlight, and then again when the sun came up?"

Sabena was drowning in her desire for him. It would be so easy to give in, to let him bring her untold ecstasy.

But she couldn't settle for that, knowing that some day it would be over and her world would fall apart. There was only one way to make him stop tormenting her. The truth. She took a deep breath.

"It won't work, Jake, because I made the mistake of falling in love with you. I know that's not something you want to hear. You told me exactly how you feel about love and commitments. I don't expect you to change your mind, but one-sided love is too painful." Her lashes swept down so she wouldn't have to watch the desire drain out of his face.

Jake's reaction was totally unexpected. Instead of releasing her, his arms tightened, crushing her against his hard body. She looked up to find him staring at her with blazing eyes.

"Sweet, maddening Sabena," he said huskily. "Why did I have to drag the truth out of you?"

"You knew all along?" she asked uncertainly.

"If I only had! You put me through hell, never knowing when you'd leave me for good."

She stared at him searchingly. "Would you really have minded? You said you didn't need anybody."

He smoothed her cheek tenderly. "I never did before I met you. I didn't know that love could make every day special. That just the sound of your voice could touch my heart."

"You love me?" she whispered.

He laughed out of sheer delight. "What do you think I've been telling you? Will you marry me, sweetheart? I quite simply can't live without you."

Sabena smiled enchantingly. "I'll marry you any time, any place."

Tiny lights flickered in Jake's topaz eyes as he lifted her in his arms. "Can we iron out the details later?"

"Much later," Sabena murmured, parting her lips for his kiss.

* * * * *

**Silhouette Books
is proud to present
our best authors,
their best books...
and the best in
your reading pleasure!**

Throughout 1993, look for exciting books
by these top names in contemporary
romance:

CATHERINE COULTER—
Aftershocks in February

FERN MICHAELS—
Whisper My Name in March

DIANA PALMER—
Heather's Song in March

ELIZABETH LOWELL—
Love Song for a Raven in April

SANDRA BROWN
(previously published under
the pseudonym Erin St. Claire)—
Led Astray in April

LINDA HOWARD—
All That Glitters in May

When it comes to passion,
we wrote the book.

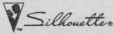

BOBT1R

Take 4 bestselling love stories FREE

Plus get a FREE surprise gift!

It takes a very special man to win

She's friend, wife, mother—she's you! And beside each Special Woman stands a wonderfully *special* man. It's a celebration of our heroines—and the men who become part of their lives.

Look for these exciting titles from Silhouette Special Edition:

January **BUILDING DREAMS** by Ginna Gray

February **HASTY WEDDING** by Debbie Macomber

March **THE AWAKENING** by Patricia Coughlin

April **FALLING FOR RACHEL** by Nora Roberts

Dont miss THAT SPECIAL WOMAN! each month—from your special authors.

AND

For the most special woman of all—you, our loyal reader—we have a wonderful gift: a beautiful journal to record all of your special moments. See this month's THAT SPECIAL WOMAN! title for details.

TSW1